RAMOSE

PRINCE IN EXILE

CAROLE WILKINSON

CATNIP BOOKS
Published by Catnip Publishing Ltd.
Islington Business Centre
3-5 Islington High Street
London N1 9LQ

This edition published 2006
1 3 5 7 9 10 8 6 4 2

First published in Australia in 2001 by black dog books,
71 Gertrude Street, Fitzroy Vic 3065

A CIP catalogue record for this book is available from the
British Library

ISBN 10: 1 84647 000 5
ISBN 13: 978 1 84647 000 4

Printed in Poland

CONTENTS

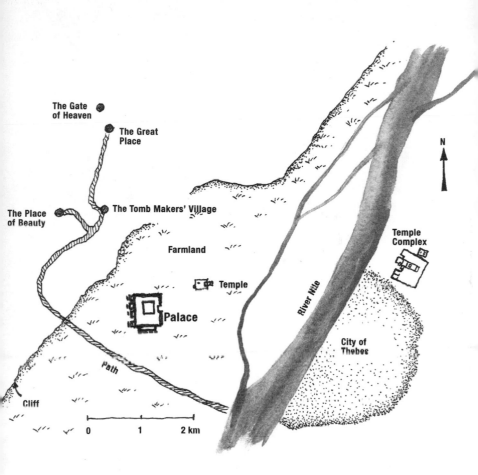

The Gate
of Heaven

The Great
Place

The Tomb Makers' Village

The Place
of Beauty

Farmland

Temple

Palace

Path

Cliff

0   1   2 km

River Nile

Temple
Complex

City of
Thebes

N

PHARAOH'S HEIR

THE BOY was standing on a dry, rocky hill. He looked around. There wasn't a blade of anything growing. He looked down at himself. Why were his clothes so dusty and why was he wearing such awful reed sandals? Where were his red leather ones with the turned-up toes? He heard a mournful chanting drifting up from below. Snaking along in the valley was a

procession. At the front was a jackal-headed priest. The sun reflected on gold and jewels. A beautiful coffin on an ornate sled was being pulled by six oxen. Six priests followed behind. They all wore brilliant white robes with leopard skins draped over their shoulders.

It was a funeral procession. The boy looked closer. How many loads of funeral goods were there? How many mourners were there?

He had a special interest in this funeral.

It was his own.

Ramose awoke and shivered. He hoped it was a dream, but he was too scared to open his eyes. What if it wasn't? He opened one eye. He could see something green. He opened the other eye. He could see something blue. He sighed with relief. He was in his sleeping chamber. Above him was the bright coloured wall painting of his father hunting a hippopotamus. His father was standing on a papyrus boat about to throw a spear. The river beneath the boat teemed with fish and eels. The unfortunate hippopotamus, unaware of his fate, wallowed in the mud at the water's edge. The reeds growing on the river bank were full of birds and butterflies. On the other wall was a painting of the blue-skinned god Amun.

Ramose had woken up to these paintings all his life and he loved them. He didn't see his father

very often in the flesh, but he had the painting to look at, and Amun, king of the gods, was always there watching over him while he slept.

Through the window Ramose could see the date palms and tamarisk trees in his own private courtyard. He got up from his bed and walked outside. The air was already warm even though it was early. He climbed up the stone stairs to the roof. The white-walled palace buildings spread in front of him.

Ramose breathed in deeply. A familiar smell filled his nostrils, the damp, slightly rotting smell of the fields to the east where all the palace food was grown. Beyond the palace walls, beyond the gardens, was the silver, glittering strip of the Nile. On the other side of the river was the sprawling city of Thebes and, to the north, the temple complex with towering obelisks and colourful pennants fluttering from gold-tipped flagpoles.

Ramose climbed back down again. Two servants were waiting to dress him in a clean white kilt and a tunic—both made of fine linen. They brought him fresh bread, sweet cake filled with dried plums and pomegranate juice for his breakfast. He sat down on an elegant chair with legs that ended in carved lion's feet. He chewed on the bread while the servants put on his sandals.

"Not those," he said kicking away the brown sandals the servant was putting on his feet.

"I want the red leather ones with the turned-up toes."

One of the servants spilt a few drops of juice on the floor.

"You're a clumsy fool," said Ramose crossly. "And this bread is too hard. Tell the baker I like it softer."

Heria came in with Topi, his pet monkey. The animal screeched, ran over and snatched the bread from his mouth. Ramose laughed.

"I dreamt I was watching my own funeral procession, Heria." Ramose's smile faded as he remembered his dream again. "What does that mean?" Heria was the royal children's nanny. She had also been their father's nanny. She was now an old woman with greying hair. Heria knew all about dreams.

"Dreaming of your own death is a good omen," said the old woman fiddling with the small flask-shaped amulet she always wore around her neck. "It means you will have long life." She smiled fondly at the boy.

Ramose was relieved. Heria had once kept him away from the river for a month because he'd dreamt that he was drinking a cup of green water. She'd thought that was a very bad dream that meant he would die from drowning.

"Haven't you finished yet?" Ramose snapped at the servant who was combing his hair. He

pushed the servant away roughly and took Topi in his arms. The monkey wrapped its tail around Ramose's arm like a furry bracelet.

Ramose went out into the corridor. He was in the mood for a game. He entered the western hall. It contained nothing but six enormous stone columns made of red granite brought all the way from Kush. They were so big that three men clasping hands wouldn't have been able to reach around one of them. The columns reached high above him, higher than the palm trees. Their tops were decorated to look like giant papyrus reeds, but painted bright colours: red, blue and yellow. Ramose didn't feel dwarfed by the giant columns. He'd been walking beneath them all his life.

The palace was a lonely place these days. His father was away on a campaign in Kush, or was it Punt? Ramose's father was away on campaigns most of the time and Ramose often forgot exactly where he was. And his brothers. His brothers were gone.

Wadzmose, his elder brother had died in a chariot accident three years ago while he was doing military service in Memphis, the city in the north of Egypt. Amenmose, who had been only a year older than Ramose, had got some sort of stomach sickness after eating stuffed ibex and had died the year before. His mother was only a distant memory. Now there was only him and

his sister, Hatshepsut. Apart from Tuthmosis of course, his snivelling little half-brother and the brat's ugly mother, Mutnofret. They kept to their own part of the palace, thank Amun. Hopefully they'd soon be going to the women's palace at Abu Ghurob for the winter months.

The only people he passed in the hall were servants. They all looked down as they passed him. They weren't allowed to look into his eyes. He liked to turn towards them quickly, so that he could catch them out. If they did look him in the eye, they had to get down on their knees and beg his forgiveness.

He came to his sister's apartments. She was still in her robing room.

"Come and play with me, Penu," he called out to his sister, using the nickname he called her by, which meant "mouse".

"I'm too old for games," she replied from the depths of her rooms. "Go and play with your silly monkey."

Ramose was about to go in and pull her hair, but one of his sister's companions stopped him.

"You can't go into your sister's chamber," she said.

Ramose didn't argue. His sister's companions were sterner than the guards. They weren't servants, but daughters of his father's officials and they treated Hatshepsut as if she was a

delicate vase that would easily break. He left his sister's rooms.

By the time he reached the eastern hall, Ramose would have welcomed any company, anyone to talk to—anyone except Vizier Wersu whom he saw walking towards him. Ramose quickly ducked behind a column. Wersu was the most important man in Egypt after the pharaoh. Ramose didn't like him. He was tall and thin with bony hands that felt like large insects when they touched you. He had a thin-lipped mouth full of small sharp teeth. The vizier reminded Ramose of a crocodile. He usually sat quietly in the background, but he could turn dangerous at the blink of an eye.

"Good morning," said a deep, growling voice. Ramose jumped. Wersu had come up behind him. Ramose sometimes thought the vizier had eyes that could see through stone. "I hope Your Highness had a restful night."

His thin mouth smiled, but his eyes held a different message. They told Ramose that the vizier didn't really wish that he'd had a restful night at all. It was almost as if he knew about his nightmare. Topi growled. He didn't like Wersu either.

"I slept extremely well, Vizier. I'm most refreshed."

Ramose continued down the corridor and out into the garden. He sat by the lotus pool

while Topi ran up the palm trees to get dates. Remembering his dream had made Ramose feel uneasy. Keneben, Ramose's tutor, came into the garden. He was a young man with a pleasant face that was usually smiling.

"It's time for your lessons, Highness," he said bowing to the boy.

Ramose liked his tutor a lot, but that didn't mean that he liked his lessons.

"I'm not doing any lessons today," Ramose said, folding his arms crossly. "I want to go down to the river to fish instead."

"Your lessons are very important, Prince Ramose," said Keneben patiently.

"Why? They're dull."

"Pharaoh's heir must be wise."

Ramose still wasn't used to the idea that he would be pharaoh one day. When he was young it had always been his brothers who had to shoulder that burden. He had been free to play with the other palace boys, the sons of his father's officials. Now that both his brothers were dead, the burden was his.

"I don't need to be able to read and write. I just need to learn to hunt and command an army like my father," Ramose complained. "You know I'll have hundreds of scribes to do all the reading and writing for me."

"It would never do for your scribes to be more

knowledgeable than you, Highness," Keneben replied. "Even the vizier should not be more scholarly than the pharaoh."

Ramose didn't mind about the scribes, but he definitely wanted to be smarter than Wersu. Keneben knew he'd won the argument. He smiled and walked towards the schoolroom. Ramose followed him.

THE SCHOOLROOM

PRINCE RAMOSE was a clever boy. He could read the hieroglyphs that were only used for writing on the walls of tombs and temples. He could also read the cursive handwriting that the scribes used for keeping records. He could add up numbers in his head without writing them down. The prince also had a good knowledge of the history of Egypt. He knew

the names of all the pharaohs going back to the beginning of time.

There was one thing Ramose wasn't good at though and that was writing. He knew all the words, but when he wrote them down on a papyrus, no one could read them. His writing was untidy and the lines of script wandered up and down the scroll, like beetle trails in the sand. He could never get the right amount of ink on his reed pen. There was either too much and the letters merged into fat inky blobs or there wasn't enough and they were thin and too pale to read. Keneben tried to encourage him to practise every day.

Ramose sat on the floor with his kilt stretched over his crossed knees to make a writing surface. Princess Hatshepsut came into the schoolroom followed by two of her companions. Ramose smiled at his sister. She didn't sit on a reed mat on the floor. She took her place on a chair carved with lotuses, straightening her dress around her and arranging her long hair until she looked like one of the goddesses painted on the temple walls. She was only thirteen years old, just two years older than Ramose and still with a girlish face, but her manner was like that of a grown woman. She moved so gracefully, spoke so quietly and never wanted to do anything silly.

"Why do you come to the schoolroom every day,

Penu?" he asked his sister. "Girls don't have to learn to read and write. If I didn't have to learn, I'd be out doing something more interesting."

"I think it's important to learn the scribal skills," said Hatshepsut taking her pens and palette from her servant. "I will be married one day and my husband will be pleased to have a wife who can help him with his business affairs."

Keneben gave them both a well-worn papyrus to copy.

"Not this one again!" grumbled Ramose. "I've written this out at least fifty times."

It was a text about the benefits of being a scribe, how easy the work was compared to being a farmer or a labourer, how a scribe didn't get calluses on his hands.

Ramose was still grumbling. "I'm never going to be a scribe. What do I care whether they have to work hard or not?"

Hatshepsut didn't complain.

Ramose opened his brush container. It was made of carved ebony with a pattern inlaid in gold, ivory and turquoise. He pulled out a reed and chewed the end to make a brush. He spat out threads of reed. It was a disagreeable thing to have to do. His sister got her servants to prepare her brushes. He'd have to remember to do the same. Keneben brought him a bowl of water. Ramose dipped his brush into the water and

then rubbed it on the ink block on his palette. He started to write.

"Wait, Highness!" said Keneben. "First you must say a prayer to Thoth, god of writing, and sprinkle water in offering to him."

"That's what scribes have to do," complained Ramose. "I'm not a scribe."

Hatshepsut was muttering the prayer and sprinkling a few drops of water on her papyrus. She started to copy out the lesson. She wrote in beautiful even script, in perfect arrow-straight lines. Ramose dipped his fingers in the water and dripped too much water on his scroll. He wiped it off with his kilt and started writing.

After they had both copied the text, Keneben dipped his reed pen into his red ink ready to correct their work. On Ramose's papyrus, he crossed out words on every line, rewriting them in red in the margin.

"There is some improvement, Highness." Ramose knew Keneben was lying. "Perhaps you might like to write out some of the words again."

He was only a tutor and he couldn't actually tell the future pharaoh that he had terrible handwriting. Keneben turned to Hatshepsut's papyrus. His red pen hung above her scroll as he read it.

"Not a single mistake, Princess," he said putting down his pen unused. "And every word

is perfectly formed as always. Your writing is beautiful to behold."

Hatshepsut smiled at the tutor and he bowed to her as if she was the one complimenting him.

Ramose yawned. "I'm bored with lessons."

"You haven't practised reading hieroglyphs yet, Highness," said Keneben.

Ramose groaned as Keneben unrolled a scroll that was at least five cubits long and covered in word-pictures.

"The hieroglyphs are beautifully drawn, Keneben," Hatshepsut said.

Keneben blushed. "You are very kind, Princess."

"I'll begin reading the scroll," she said.

The text was about a battle fought by a pharaoh from an earlier dynasty. Hatshepsut read well and Ramose was soon following the story and wanting to have a turn at reading.

"It's a lot more interesting than the text about scribes," he said.

Eventually though, Ramose got bored with that as well. He uncrossed his stiff legs and stood up. He had ink spots on his kilt.

"I've had enough lessons. I'm going down to the river to play at naval battles. Do you want to come, Penu?"

His sister laughed. "I'd have skin as dark as a peasant girl's if I went outside as often as you

want me to," she said. "I prefer to stay indoors."

A few years ago she would have been as keen as Ramose to pretend the ibis were enemy soldiers and throw papyrus stalk spears at them. Now she thought Ramose's games were childish. She spent all of her time with her women companions who rubbed her pale skin with perfumed oils, tied ornaments in her hair and painted her eyelids green.

Ramose walked quickly along the path that led to the river. Three servants hurried after him. One had a fan to cool the prince if he got hot. Another carried a chair, in case he felt like sitting down. Another brought a water jar and some grapes. Ramose made one of them get into the river and pretend he was a hippopotamus so that he had something to hunt. The servant did as he was told, even though crocodiles had occasionally been seen in that part of the river.

Ramose was bored with the game after ten minutes. Not so long ago, games like that had occupied him for hours. He sank down on the lion-footed chair and sighed. Games weren't any fun when you played alone. Or else he was just getting too old for games. The thought depressed him. He stood up to throw grapes at a passing flock of ducks and slipped in the soft mud at the river's edge. Now there were mud stains as well as ink spots on his kilt. He thought he saw one of

the servants smirk to himself. Ramose felt a flash of anger.

"I'm tired," he said. "You can carry me back to the palace."

Two of the servants lifted him on the chair and carried him along the path. He made them go the long way, through the pomegranate grove and around the vegetable gardens. That would teach them to laugh at him.

Heria was waiting for him when they returned to the palace.

"It's past time for your midday meal, Prince," she said. Ramose realised that he was very hungry. He took the old woman's hand. "I feel like a pelican egg, Heria," he said.

"I'll send to the kitchens for one immediately."

Heria and Keneben sat on reed mats on the floor. They would only eat when their prince had finished. Ramose sat down on a stool. A servant girl placed plates of food next to him on a low table.

"I'll have a little gazelle meat and bread while I wait for the pelican egg," he said. Heria held the plates up to him. He picked up the food with his fingers.

"Where's Topi?" he said raising the meat to his mouth.

Heria suddenly screamed. Keneben leapt to his feet and launched himself at Ramose. He slapped

the boy's hand away from his mouth just as he
was about to eat the gazelle meat.

Ramose looked at his tutor in amazement.
"What do you think you're doing?" he demanded
angrily.

Heria was trembling. Her bony finger was
pointing at a lump on the floor. Ramose looked
closer. The lump was brown and furry. It was
Topi. The boy fell to his knees next to his pet.

"What's wrong with him?" He picked up the
animal's limp body. The monkey's tongue was
lolling out of its mouth. "He's dead. Topi's dead."

He looked around at his tutor and his nanny
for explanation. They were both grim faced.
Heria took the amulet from around her neck
and handed it to Keneben. He broke a seal from
the top. The amulet was actually a small flask.
Keneben grabbed hold of Ramose roughly.

"What are you doing? I'll call the guards!"

The tutor's mouth was severe. He didn't answer.
His eyes had a fierce determined look that Ramose
didn't recognise. Ramose was afraid—afraid for
his life. Keneben forced the neck of the flask to
Ramose's lips and tipped the contents into his
mouth. He grabbed the boy's hair and pulled his
head back so that he had no choice but to swallow.
Ramose was surprised at the strength in his
tutor's hands. He felt the bitter-tasting liquid run
down his throat. He broke out of Keneben's hold

and got to his feet. Ramose's legs felt strange. They crumpled beneath him. The room was spinning. Heria was wailing. He could hear the birds in the courtyard calling. The sounds grew further and further away. The faces of his tutor and his nanny grew smaller. He opened his mouth to ask them what they had done to him. Then the floor came up and slapped him in the face.

AFTERLIFE

RAMOSE AWOKE and shivered. He hoped it was a dream, but he was too scared to open his eyes. What if it wasn't? He opened one eye. He could see nothing. He felt like he wanted to be sick. He opened the other eye. Everything was still black. He couldn't see a thing, but he could smell something. The salty smell of natron, the stuff that the priests used to preserve bodies

before they were mummified. There was also the sharp, sweet smell of juniper oil which was poured over the body after it was wrapped in linen strips. He was lying on a cold stone table. This is no dream, thought Ramose. His stomach turned somersaults. I'm dead. Someone is about to cut open my body, take out my insides and turn me into a mummy. Ramose heard someone moving. He raised his head. There was a figure in the corner leaning over a lamp.

"You're awake!" said a familiar voice.

"Heria!" said Ramose. "Did you die too?"

"You're not dead, Highness."

"But this is a tomb isn't it?"

Heria shook her head, helped Ramose to sit up and gave him some cool water to drink.

"This is an embalming room beneath the temple of Maat," said the old woman.

Ramose was confused. His mind was still foggy. He was lying on the stone table made especially for embalming dead people. He could see the channels that were meant to carry away the blood when the dead bodies were cut open with a sharp flint. What am I doing in an embalming room if I'm not dead, thought Ramose. He drank the water and then immediately vomited it up again. Heria stroked his back the way she always did when he was sick.

"What's happened to me, Heria?"

Ramose was trying to remember what had happened. Something frightening, something so bad his brain was keeping it hidden from him.

Keneben came into the room and bowed to the prince.

"I hope you're feeling better, Highness," he said.

Ramose suddenly remembered the tutor's strong grip and the taste of the bitter liquid. He looked from his tutor to his nanny. The two people he had trusted most in the world.

"You poisoned me," he said, trying to get to his feet.

Keneben knelt at the prince's feet. "No, Highness, I wish you nothing but health and long life."

"Someone tried to poison you, my prince, but they failed, thank Amun."

Heria sat next to Ramose and started to tell him a story. She had told him many stories in his life, but never one that scared him like this one.

"As soon as Queen Mutnofret came to the palace I knew she was trouble," the nanny said. "I never liked her. When your dear mother died Mutnofret made sure that she became Pharaoh's favourite wife. Then your half-brother was born and I guessed what her plan was. She wanted her own son to be the next pharaoh. I found a written spell in an amulet around her brat's neck. I took the spell to Keneben to find out what it meant."

Keneben continued the story. "It was a spell to bring death to you and your royal brothers, Highness. I don't believe peasant magic can kill a royal heir, but when your brother Prince Wadzmose died, I wondered if it really was an accident. When Prince Amenmose died as well, I was convinced that someone was killing the princes and that you would be next."

"Since then, we have watched you day and night," Heria said with tears in her eyes. "Poisoning was what we feared most. That's why we tested all your food on the monkey first."

All the inexplicable things started to make sense.

"Poor Topi," said Ramose. In many ways the monkey had been his best friend.

Ramose took another sip of water. This time it stayed down. Then he tried a mouthful of bread.

"When can I go back to the palace? We must send messengers to my father."

"I don't think that's wise, Highness."

"Why not? If Pharaoh knows what she's done, he'll imprison Queen Mutnofret."

"We can't prove it was her. She'll just deny it. Pharaoh is very fond of her and she has a way of making things sound convincing."

Ramose's head ached. He was finding it difficult to understand what his tutor and nanny were planning.

"But what am I to do? I can't stay here—unless you think I should become an embalmer." Ramose laughed despite the pain in his head and his somersaulting stomach. The idea of him having to work for a living was ridiculous. Keneben and Heria didn't laugh though. They didn't even smile.

"If you're to become pharaoh, Highness, you must stay hidden until you are old enough to claim the throne."

"Hidden? You mean imprisoned?"

"No, Highness."

"We have given this a lot of thought. There are so few people in the palace whom we can really trust. The vizier is more than likely on the side of the queen. He is a powerful man who no one dares to defy. Every servant and slave will be a potential enemy. It's too dangerous for you to stay in the palace."

"We could hide you somewhere in a different town—even a different country."

Ramose shuddered at the thought of leaving Egypt.

"Wherever you go, eventually word will get back to the vizier and the queen."

"The only way that you will be safe is if everyone thinks you're dead."

"The potion you drank, Highness, gave you every appearance of being dead."

Heria wept again at the memory. "When you were taken away for embalming, I managed to switch your body with that of a peasant boy about your age who had just died of an illness."

"Does my father think I am dead? My sister?"

"Yes. It was the only way to ensure your safety."

"But surely you don't expect me to stay here?" Ramose said, indicating the dusty, smelly room.

"No, Highness, of course not," said Keneben. "What I have in mind is that you disguise yourself as an apprentice scribe."

"An apprentice scribe!"

"Yes, Highness," said Heria. "You won't need to do physical work, and you have the scribal skills."

"I have found a scribe looking for an apprentice. He and his wife have no children. They are looking for a boy to train to take the scribe's place."

"I won't become a scribe," shouted Ramose. "I'm Pharaoh's son, the heir to the throne of Egypt. I won't do it. You can't make me!"

THE EDGE OF
THE WORLD

RAMOSE LEANED over the side of the papyrus boat and trailed his hand in the blue river water. An old man was rowing the boat across the Nile, the life-blood of Egypt. Without the river Egypt would not exist, he knew that. The river gave Egyptians water to drink and to make their crops grow. Each year in the season of akhet the river turned green and flooded. The

fields disappeared beneath its waters. When the water receded and the Nile shrank back to its normal size, a layer of black silt was left over all the farmland. It was a gift from the gods that made fruit and vegetables grow fat and full of flavour.

Ramose knew these things because Keneben had taught him. He cupped some of the Nile water in his hand and drank it.

The small boat reached the western bank of the river and Ramose climbed out. He was wearing a coarse tunic over his kilt. He still had his favourite red leather sandals though. He had insisted on keeping them.

The path from the river skirted around the palace. Behind those walls, which were almost close enough to touch, were his sister, his tutor and his dear nanny. Maybe his father was also there, just returned from a triumphant campaign in Kush. But as well as the people who loved him, there were also people who wished him dead—the queen, the vizier and the brat-prince, Tuthmosis.

Ramose walked on without stopping. There was no one to farewell him as he walked away from the places that were familiar to him. The day before, Heria and Keneben had sneaked away from the palace at different times to say goodbye to him. It was too risky for him to be seen with either of them and they didn't trust anyone to guide him.

Instead, Keneben had drawn a map for the prince on a small sheet of papyrus.

Ramose walked along a path between a canal and fields of wheat and vegetables. The path was shaded by date palms. Peasant farmers went about their daily business without even glancing at him. The path zigzagged past fig trees and grape vines. A man lifted water from a canal and poured it into his fields using a device with a leather bucket at the end of a counter-balanced pole. He carefully watered each melon vine and every onion plant. Ramose breathed in the moist air laden with the heavy smell of ripe fruit, lotus flowers and animal dung.

Then the fields ended abruptly as if someone had drawn a line in the earth. There were no more irrigation canals. The desert began just as suddenly as the fields had ended. And the path immediately changed from a smooth, well-travelled roadway to a rough, sandy track with no trees to shade it. The familiar smells of the Egypt he knew faded and the hot, dry smell-less air of the desert filled his nostrils.

Ramose had never walked in the desert before. It was a dangerous place, inhabited only by barbarians, sand dwellers and the dead. The path started to climb. On either side there was nothing but hot sand—apart from the rock that Ramose managed to fall headlong over. He picked

up the rock and threw it angrily down the cliff. It skipped and bounced down the rock face. If Ramose had been in the palace he would have blamed a servant for leaving something in his way for him to fall over. He would have yelled abuse at the servant and that would have made him feel better. Ramose watched the rock smash into a dozen pieces when it hit the bottom. It made him feel worse.

Ramose sat in the sand and had to concentrate hard to stop himself from crying. Normally if he so much as knocked his knee against a stool, three servants would have been at his side to see if he needed attention. A priest would have been called to say a prayer for him. There he was, sprawled in the dirt and no one came to help him. He was alone for the first time in his life. The harsh sun burned the back of his neck. Ramose looked up at the path that rose steeply in front of him. He got to his feet and walked on. He had a long way to go.

The hill turned into a steep cliff and the path zigzagged back and forth sharply in order to find a way up. Jagged stones dug into his sandals as he climbed. Ramose adjusted the bag on his shoulder. It was a small bag made of woven reeds—the sort that peasants carried their food to the fields in. Yet at that moment the simple bag contained all Ramose's possessions.

He reached the top of the cliff and sat down panting. He looked back the way he had come, shading his eyes from the sun. In the distance, he could see the glittering ribbon of the Nile with a stripe of green on each side. He was shocked to see what a thin strip of fertility Egypt was, clinging to the edges of the Nile. The hostile desert beyond stretched as far as the eye could see on either side of it. At the river's edge, he could just make out the whitewashed walls of the palace. On the other side was the sprawling city and the temple complex with its flags flying and its gold glinting in the sunlight. That was where he had spent the last two weeks, hidden in a basement room. He turned away from the Nile, away from the land he had known all his life, walked over the crest of the hill and down into a valley.

Ramose couldn't imagine why the desert was called the Red Land, when it all seemed to be a dirty yellow colour. The slope below him was covered in sharp rocks and flints where a cliff had long ago collapsed. He could just make out a mud brick village on the valley floor the same colour as the desert hills around it. If he hadn't been looking for it, he might not have even seen the village. From a distance it could easily have been a natural feature, shaped by the winds. There was no green, no gold, no sign of life. This was his new home—the village of the tomb makers.

Over the next hill, he knew, was the Great Place, the valley that his father had chosen for his tomb and for the tombs of future pharaohs. It was a special place, a place sacred to the gods, where Pharaoh hoped his tomb would be safe from tomb robbers.

Ramose had refused to leave the city at first. As a prince he was used to getting his own way. But the more he'd thought about it, the more he knew Heria and Keneben were right. He wouldn't be safe in the palace. Queen Mutnofret was a strong-willed and powerful woman who was feared by servants and officials alike. Eventually Ramose had agreed to their plan. He would live secretly as an apprentice scribe until Keneben and Heria could find proof of Queen Mutnofret's treachery against him and his brothers. They would seek out the people who had provided the poison, the ones who had rigged his brother's chariot accident and buy the truth with gold. It would be no more than six months, they said.

Keneben had found a scribe called Paneb in the tomb makers' village who was looking for a boy to take on as an apprentice. The scribe had had a local boy in mind for the job, but a large sum in gold and copper had convinced him that Ramose would be a better choice.

Ramose rehearsed his new life story in his head as he walked. He had been born in a distant part

of Egypt far to the south. He was the son of a local official and had been trained to follow in his father's footsteps. A terrible disease had swept the town though, and both his parents had died. He had miraculously survived and been brought up by an uncle in the city. The uncle had recently died too, leaving him with no one to care for him. Ramose hoped he'd got all the details right.

THE RED LAND

THE TOMB MAKERS' village didn't look very welcoming. A high mud brick wall surrounded it. There was just one entrance. Ramose was exhausted. The journey from the city had taken less than two hours, but the prince had never walked so far in his life. It was past noon and he was hungry and thirsty.

There was one street in the village and it was

empty. It hardly even deserved to be called a street. It was just the space between two rows of houses. Keneben's map showed the scribe's house about halfway along the street and on the left-hand side. There weren't that many houses, the whole village would have fitted into one corner of the palace.

Ramose was soon standing outside the house with Paneb's name inscribed above the door. Even though he was tired and hungry, he had a strong urge to turn and run all the way back to the palace and tell Keneben that he'd changed his mind. The door suddenly opened and a small figure burst out and nearly knocked him over. It was a young girl.

Ramose stared at her. He couldn't help it. Her skin was as dark as Nile mud. She had large rings in her ears and a string of fat orange beads around her neck. Her hair was a mass of tight black curls. She wore a length of coarse-looking material with broad stripes in green and red over her head. Around her waist was a strange belt made of intricately folded cloth. She glared back at Ramose.

"What are you staring at?"

No one had ever spoken to Ramose in that way before. He opened his mouth to call for the guards and have the girl taken away. He closed his mouth again, standing on the doorstep in

confusion. The girl looked him up and down, at his broken sandals, dusty garment and sweating face.

"The boy's here," she called over her shoulder and then she ran off down the street.

A man appeared at the doorway.

"You're late," he said. "We were expecting you earlier."

Paneb wasn't at all like Ramose had imagined him. He'd had a vague picture in his head of a younger man who smiled a lot, someone like Keneben. The scribe was an old man, much older than Ramose's father, his hair was grey, his skin lined and he was fat. His stomach hung over his kilt and he had a number of chins.

"I was held up at the river," Ramose lied.

"You better come in."

Three steps led down from the street into the scribe's house. The house was so narrow, Ramose felt that if he stretched out his arms he could have touched both walls at once. The scribe led him into a room where two women were waiting. One was Ianna, the scribe's wife, the other was Teti, their servant.

"This is Ramose," Paneb told the women.

"The same name as the poor prince," said Ianna, who was fat like her husband.

Ramose nodded. Heria had wanted him to take another name, but he thought he might lose

himself completely if he didn't at least have his real name.

"Such a sad thing for a boy to die so young," she said.

"Very unfortunate," said Paneb. "Such a rush to get his tomb ready."

The servant brought in a tray of food.

"We've already eaten our midday meal," said the scribe. "But you're probably hungry after your journey."

Ramose was hungry. He watched as the servant put bread and meat, cooked vegetables and fruit on a low table. It was a small amount of food that had obviously been picked over already and then left uncovered to dry out. Several flies circled the food. The meat was from a pig. Ramose had never eaten anything but the best quality beef. If he'd been at the palace he would have kicked over the table and demanded fresh food. He was very hungry though.

Ramose sat and waited for Teti to serve him and to pour something for him to drink. She didn't move. There was an awkward silence. Paneb and his wife watched him with puzzled expressions. "Is there something wrong?" asked Ianna.

"No," said Ramose.

He looked at the food. The others looked at him. Ramose suddenly realised that he had to serve

himself. He moved over to the table and helped himself to the food. The bread was gritty and the meat was tough. All there was to drink was beer, which had a bitter taste.

"May I have some gazelle's milk?" he asked. He was pleased that he had remembered to ask politely instead of demanding it.

The servant looked surprised and shook her head. Paneb and his wife exchanged doubtful looks. Ramose ate his meal in silence.

When he had finished the meagre meal, the servant brought him a bowl of water to wash his hands. He had to be grateful for small blessings.

"Where is my room?" he asked the scribe.

"You don't have a room," Paneb replied. "You will sleep on the roof. My wife has a chest for you to keep your things in."

Ramose had never been in an ordinary house before. It was tiny, just three rooms and an outdoor kitchen. There was only one bedroom and that was where Paneb and his wife slept. The servant woman and the girl slept out in the garden.

Teti carried the chest up to the roof for Ramose. The chest wasn't made of wood but woven from date palm leaves. It was rather old and the leather hinges didn't look too strong. Ramose unpacked his few possessions and put them in the trunk. All that Heria and Keneben had allowed him to bring

was a spare kilt, some scratchy undergarments and a woollen cloak. Keneben had given him some gold shaped into large ring-shaped ingots in case of emergencies. He hid them under everything else. He also put his scribe's kit in the chest. He realised that his own ebony brush box and palette, inlaid with ivory, gold and turquoise, would be too rich for a humble scribe. He would have to pretend he had lost his scribe's tools and ask Paneb to provide new ones.

Paneb, like the other workers, worked an eight-day shift at the pharaoh's tomb, followed by two days rest. This was his second rest day, he would be returning to work the next day. That gave Ramose the rest of the afternoon to explore the house and the village. Half an hour would have been enough really. It took ten minutes to walk the length of the one street. The fifteen or so houses were built squashed up against each other and all looked the same.

Outside the village walls there was a small temple, a half-finished building almost as large as the village and a lot of sand and rocks.

What was there to amuse a boy in this miserable place? There were no gardens, no ponds, no orchards, no river. No animals to hunt, no fish to catch. A group of boys about the same age as Ramose were playing a game that involved drawing lines in the sand. It looked very dull.

They all looked at him as he walked by, but no one spoke.

When he got back to the scribe's house, he wondered what he was going to do with himself for the rest of the day. Wandering around, he found the dark-skinned girl out in the garden. She was on her hands and knees grinding grain on a curved stone.

"So you're the new apprentice," she said.

"And who are you?" Ramose demanded.

"My name is Karoya," she said, "I grind the grain." She sprinkled more wheat grains on the curved surface and rolled a round stone back and forth over them.

"You're a slave, aren't you," said Ramose. "Are you from Kush?"

"Yes. Not that it's any business of yours."

"I don't think you should talk to me like that," said Ramose.

"Why not?"

Ramose didn't know what to say to this insolent girl.

"Where I come from you'd be beaten for such rudeness."

"And who's going to beat me?" laughed Karoya. "Certainly not a puny little apprentice scribe, like you. You'd have to catch me first."

"Where are the rest of the servants?" asked Ramose changing the subject.

"There aren't any more servants, just Teti and me."

"But who will dress me? Who will help me bathe?"

"Who will dress you?" Karoya stopped grinding and looked up at him in amazement. "Only babies can't dress themselves."

Ramose looked at the shocked expression on the girl's face and realised he'd made another mistake.

"I was just joking," he said, and went back into the house. Ramose didn't like making mistakes. He didn't like having to pretend he was an ordinary person. There was nothing about his new life that he liked.

Ramose had been looking forward to washing off the dust and sweat from his walk. Water was precious out there in the desert. He was only allowed to have two jars of water to bathe with. It was such a small amount of water. He was also given a tiny jar of animal fat mixed with limestone to cleanse his skin. He knocked over one of the jars, spilling most of the water meant for rinsing, leaving his skin covered with the chalky fat. So much for bathing, thought Ramose. I probably smell worse now than I did before.

That night Ramose lay on his back. Then he lay on his left side. Next he tried his right side. It didn't

matter which way he lay he just couldn't get comfortable. How could he? How could anybody be expected to sleep lying out on the roof on a rickety old bed with a base of woven reeds? He'd only been given one thin blanket. Nights in the desert were cold. Even wrapped in his cloak he was freezing.

Ramose was still awake when the sun rose. His body, used to soft beds, was sore from head to toe. He was itchy as well. When he inspected his legs and arms, he saw that they were covered in bites. Whether they were from the mosquitoes that had buzzed around his head all night or from the fleas he had found in the blanket, he wasn't sure.

He put on his kilt. He fumbled with the ties. When he had finished it hung unevenly. He wrapped it the other way and it hung a little better, though he was sure he wouldn't be able to undo the knot he'd tied.

Breakfast was the same gritty bread and a few overripe figs.

"I'd prefer some sweet plum cake," he said to Teti.

She blinked at him as if he'd asked for a slice of the moon.

Scribe Paneb and his wife came in for their breakfast. They grabbed at the food with both hands, filling their mouths. Ianna talked and ate at the same time. Ramose suddenly lost his

appetite. He went back up to the roof, where he found the slave girl just lifting the lid of his chest.

"Take your hands off my belongings!" shouted Ramose.

"I was just going to tidy them for you," said the girl.

"Your job is to grind grain and make bread, not to touch my personal things. You were looking for something to steal, I know. My father told me that people from Kush were all thieves and barbarians!"

"I wasn't stealing anything," retorted Karoya. "Why would I want to steal your spare kilt and your undergarments?"

Ramose marched down the stairs. The scribe was still eating his breakfast.

"I found the slave girl up on the roof trying to steal my possessions," Ramose said to Paneb. "I want her punished."

"I've told her before about being inquisitive," said the scribe belching softly.

"Inquisitive!" shouted Ramose. "She's a thief. She should be beaten."

"I don't think that will be necessary," said Ianna. "She can't work as hard if she's bruised and sore."

"She can go without her evening meal," said the scribe.

Ramose couldn't understand why the scribe was being so lenient with the girl.

"It's hard to punish someone who has nothing," observed the scribe.

Ramose turned on his heel and went back up the stairs two at a time.

"That's it," he said to himself as he rammed his belongings back into the reed bag. "I'm leaving!'

PHARAOH'S TOMB

RAMOSE HAD had enough. He couldn't stay in that place with those people. He just couldn't. He strode down the village street. How could he be expected to live in such a squalid little house with such disrespectful people? He'd rather eat the palace scraps than their awful food. He'd have to explain to Heria and Keneben. It just wasn't right for a prince to have to sleep on

a flea-ridden bed out in the open and to have to put up with barbarians trying to steal what few possessions he had. It was too much.

Ramose slung his bag on his shoulder and walked out of the village gate. Worrying about being stabbed or poisoned would be much easier than living in that horrible place. He missed his sister, he missed Keneben and Heria, he missed the river, he missed being waited on. He got ten strides away from the village when a voice called out.

"Where do you think you're going?"

Ramose turned round. It was the slave girl, Karoya. She was sitting in the shade under the wall of the half-built mud brick building outside the village.

"I'm going home," Ramose replied continuing to stride away from the village. "Away from thieves and fat scribes."

"I thought you were an orphan and you didn't have a home."

"I mean the city," said Ramose still walking.

"Why would you want to go to that noisy, smelly place?"

"The part I lived in wasn't noisy and smelly."

"I thought your uncle died and you had no one to care for you."

Ramose stopped walking. He imagined returning to the palace. The only people he could really

depend upon were his sister and two servants. The queen and the vizier wanted him dead. Everyone believed he was dead already. He might not survive there for half an hour. He sat down in the sand.

"I hate the desert."

"I love the desert," said Karoya.

"There's nothing in the desert to love. Nothing but sand and rocks."

"It's beautiful. It reminds me of my home. I come out here every morning to watch the sunrise. The sky turns pink and orange and purple."

Ramose looked up at the early morning sky. The colours were beautiful, like a temple painting. Voices were drifting from the village. The first tomb workers were dawdling out of the gate, talking quietly to themselves as they headed off to work.

"I want to go home," said Ramose sadly.

"This is your home now. You just have to get used to it."

"Don't tell me what I have to do! You have no idea what I've been through."

"I know what it's like to have to leave your home and live in a foreign place full of strangers," said the girl.

Ramose sighed and leaned against the wall. "What's this building for?" he asked.

"It's a house for Pharaoh," said Karoya.

"A palace?" Ramose looked at the rough half-finished walls. "This is nothing like a palace."

"It's supposed to be for the pharaoh if he ever comes to visit. The men work on it from time to time."

"Why would Pharaoh ever want to come to this awful place?"

Karoya shrugged. "So are you leaving?"

"No."

It was now fully light.

"The scribe will be looking for you," said Karoya. "Go and wait for him at the gate. He'll think you were keen to get started."

"I don't know why you think I should take the advice of a thief," Ramose grumbled bitterly.

"I'm not a thief," said Karoya.

Ramose went over to the gate to wait for the scribe.

Paneb walked in silence. Ramose was grateful. He didn't want to talk to the scribe. He followed Paneb up the hill to the west of the village, further into the desert, further away from his home. The overweight scribe was soon puffing and panting. The other workers disappeared over the crest before Paneb and Ramose were halfway up.

The path looked the same as the one that had brought him to the village—just a dusty track worn by the passage of feet. On either side of the path was the same dry sand and sharp rocks and

flints. There were no trees, no plants, no sign of animal life. Ramose thought it must surely be the most inhospitable place in the world. They reached the top and the heat of the sun hit Ramose full in the face. He wasn't used to being outside in the heat without servants to fan him. He hoped he would be able to work out in the sun without fainting.

Ramose shielded his eyes. The Great Place lay below them. It didn't look great at all. It was a dry and sand-coloured valley the same as the valley where the village was. The only difference was the cliffs leading down to this valley floor were still standing.

"Is this it?" asked Ramose. "Where's Pharaoh's tomb?"

"Hidden underground, of course," said Paneb. "The entrance is over there."

He pointed to a hole in the side of the valley wall opposite. Ramose was disappointed. He knew that the royal tomb was being built underground to protect it from tomb robbers, but he had expected it to have an ornate entrance and elaborate temples above ground. There was nothing.

The path wove up and down until it found a way down around the cliffs. When they reached the valley floor, Ramose could see the entrance more clearly. It was just a large square hole cut

into the rock face. Outside were blocks of stone quarried from the tomb. The tomb makers were nowhere to be seen. Paneb muttered grumpily to himself as he headed to the tomb entrance. An enormous man stood at the entrance. He wasn't an Egyptian, he was black-skinned, like Karoya, and very tall.

"Good morning, Scribe Paneb," said the guard.

"Morning," grumbled Paneb.

"Who is this with you?" asked the guard.

"This is my new apprentice, Ramose. Let him pass whenever he wishes."

Paneb also introduced Ramose to Samut, a sweaty man with long stringy hair who was foreman of the tomb workers. Then they were out of the sun and suddenly in darkness. They walked down a steeply sloping corridor that led deep inside the rock. Small oil lamps lit the way at intervals, but it was still very dark. Ramose was surprised. He wasn't really sure what a scribe attached to a royal tomb was meant to do, but he'd imagined that he would be working out in the blazing sun. It had never occurred to him that he would be working deep underground.

They passed a group of sculptors working on carvings on the sloping walls of the corridor. Ramose could make out pictures of his father fighting in military campaigns. There was a carving of him firing arrows from a chariot, a

carving of him with his foot on the head of a
grovelling barbarian, another of him standing
next to a pile of dismembered hands, cut from his
victims. Hieroglyphs told the story of his bravery
and how he was undefeated in battle. The corridor
continued to slope steeply down. Ramose looked
over his shoulder. The tomb entrance was just a
small square of light high above him.

The corridor opened into a room where men
were working on the ceiling. It was painted
deep blue and the painters, clinging to a wooden
scaffold, were covering it with five-pointed yellow
stars. The murmur of voices and the sound of
the chipping of stone drifted up from a flight
of steps that led down from this room at right
angles. Ramose followed Paneb down the steps.
The burial chamber was at the bottom. Outliners
were marking out paintings and text on four
square columns supporting the ceiling. More
sculptors were on their hands and knees carving
a large red sandstone sarcophagus.

Ramose wasn't interested in the detail of the
carving though. As soon as he'd lost sight of the
square of light that was the outside, he felt panic
rise in him. He was thinking about how far it was
to the surface. He was picturing the enormous
weight of rock just above his head and imagining
it falling in and burying him alive. His breathing
started to get fast and shallow. The air was stale

and smelt of rock dust, burning oil and sweat. His skin turned icy cold. The walls were closing in on him. He was sure he was about to be crushed to death. He choked out some words.

"Outside," he stammered. "Can't breathe."

He stumbled towards the stairs, falling over a sculptor.

"Where do you think you're going?" the scribe asked impatiently. The tomb workers were all laughing.

He felt his way up the stairs. His chest felt like it was exploding. He couldn't draw a breath. He scrambled under the scaffolding, tripped over a jar of paint and crawled along the floor. A square of daylight came into view. Ramose rested his cheek on the cold stone floor and breathed in the fresh air that came from above.

"Whoever heard of a tomb worker afraid of being underground?" said one of the tomb workers. They all thought it was a great joke.

"You'll have to get used to being underground," Paneb snapped. "I can't have the workers laughing at me. You get used to it or you go."

"I'll be all right," Ramose said in a quiet, croaky voice.

"Whether you're all right or not, you have work to do," said Paneb angrily. "You must keep a tally of the copper chisels that the sculptors use."

The scribe sat down on a block of stone.

"Whenever a chisel wears out it is to be replaced.
Go back up, out to the valley and collect some new
chisels from the store. There are men up there in
the corridor with worn out chisels, we can't have
them sitting around doing nothing."

The scribe was, however, quite happy to sit and
do nothing himself.

"Where is the papyrus I am to write on?"
Ramose asked.

Paneb looked around quickly, hoping that the
workers hadn't heard.

"Where did you get this apprentice from,
Paneb?" shouted one. "Are you sure he knows
how to write?" The painters were all chuckling to
themselves.

"We don't use papyrus in the tomb," hissed
Paneb. "Whatever gave you that idea? It's very
expensive as I'm sure you know."

"So what do I write on?"

The scribe sighed at the ignorance of his
apprentice. "On stone flakes, of course. The pieces
chipped from the rock when the quarry men were
excavating the tomb. You'll find plenty of them in
piles up on the surface, all different sizes. I use
papyrus only for the documents I send to Vizier
Wersu."

Ramose shivered. Whether it was the mention
of the vizier's name or the cool air in the tomb he
wasn't sure. Either way he was glad to be making

his way out of the tomb and up into fresh air again, even if it was hot desert air.

Out on the valley floor Ramose stood in the sun and felt it heat up his skin. He looked up at the clear blue sky and the bright sun until his breathing slowed and he felt calm again. Ramose looked around the valley, now dotted with after-images of the sun. The scribe was right, there were piles of stone flakes outside the tomb entrance: small ones no bigger than a hand which could be used for short notes, larger ones for long reports.

The mud brick storehouse was about fifty paces from the tomb entrance. Another huge, dark-skinned foreigner stood on guard outside. Ramose explained who he was and the guard let him enter. The storeroom was packed with everything that the tomb makers needed: paints, tools, oil for the lamps as well as grain and water.

"Treat these very carefully," said the storekeeper taking a dozen copper chisels from a wooden chest. "The workers like their chisels sharp, and Scribe Paneb gets very angry if anybody damages them." He wrapped them carefully in a strip of linen. "One of these chisels is worth about six of those bags of wheat." He jerked his head in the direction of the food stores. "That's three months wages for you."

A boy was stacking sacks of grain. He was one

of the boys whom Ramose had seen playing a game outside the village.

Ramose took the chisels from the storeman. He walked out into the hot air again, pushing the chisels into the belt of his kilt. The other boy hurried out of the storehouse behind Ramose and knocked his elbow so that the chisels fell out of his grasp and onto the rocky ground. He didn't stop to apologise. He kept walking, turning for just long enough to give Ramose a glare full of hatred.

Ramose called out to the storeman. "Did you see that? Did you see what he did?"

A LETTER FROM HOME

THE STOREMAN shrugged and went back to his work. Ramose was furious. He took out his anger on a nearby rock. All that achieved was a bleeding toe. He collected up the scattered chisels. Three of them were damaged. He knew he'd get the blame for this.

Paneb was very angry about the damaged chisels. Ramose showed him the stone flake

on which he'd recorded the workers who had
received new chisels. Paneb wasn't very happy
about that either.

"Is that the best writing you can do?" he said
incredulously. "I can only read half of it." He
turned the stone flake around, making a big show
of how difficult it was to read. "You'll have to
rewrite it. In fact you can rewrite the whole thing
ten times to make sure you get it right."

Ramose didn't complain. He was glad to have
an excuse to get out of the tomb. He found a tiny
wedge of shade outside the tomb entrance and sat
down to rewrite the details about the chisels. He
remembered the stories that Keneben had made
him write out about how wonderful it was to be
a scribe.

"Ramose!" Paneb's voice echoed up the tomb
shaft. "Come here, boy."

So far Ramose couldn't think of anything good
about being a scribe. You might get to sit down a
lot of the time and you didn't have to lift blocks of
stone the size of small houses, but it wasn't much
fun. He trudged back down into the darkness of
the tomb past the sculptors, his heart already
starting to race at the thought of being shut off
from the light. Fortunately, Paneb only wanted a
cup of water and Ramose was soon climbing back
up the sloping corridor again. The back of his legs
ached already.

By midday Ramose had walked up and down the tomb shaft at least ten times. It seemed that every time he got to the bottom of the shaft, Paneb remembered something he wanted from above. Every time he found a patch of shade to sit down in above ground, Paneb's voice would echo up the shaft and he was needed down below.

The other workers gathered in groups to eat their midday meal. Ramose ate his gritty bread, dried fish and figs by himself. The other apprentices sat in a group of their own. He caught them looking at him a couple of times, but none of them came over to talk to him.

By the end of the day Ramose's legs ached so much and he was so tired that he just wanted to go to sleep.

"Where do we sleep?" Ramose asked Paneb when the scribe came panting up the shaft.

Paneb pointed to some piles of rocks on the valley floor opposite the storehouse. Ramose looked closer. He'd thought that they were more discarded rocks. Now he could see that they were actually low huts made from the sharp rocks that lay around on the valley floor stacked up on top of each other. The huts were roofed over with dead palm branches that must have been carried all the way up from the river.

"You can sleep with the other apprentices," Paneb said. "I can't have you in my hut. I don't

sleep well and the sound of unfamiliar breathing would keep me awake."

The three boys were sitting outside their hut.

"Scribe Paneb said I should share your hut," Ramose told them.

No one replied. Ramose went inside. The flea-ridden bed back at the scribe's house now seemed like the height of comfort. His chamber in the palace with the painted walls and the bed with the soft mattress was a dim memory. All he had to sleep on was a reed mat spread on the bare ground. He was too tired to eat. He just wanted to close his eyes. He got out his cloak and wrapped himself up in it, even though the sun had barely set.

The other boys had different ideas though. After they had eaten, they came inside the hut and played board games. Ramose had played similar games back at the palace with Keneben. It had always been a quiet business. The games the boys played involved a lot of shouting and disputing. One of the boys was a bad loser. He always accused the others of cheating, but he would do anything to win himself. Whenever Ramose was about to drift off to sleep, one of the boys would shout out or nudge him with a foot. When they were ready to sleep, they each took it in turns to keep Ramose awake while the others slept. Ramose hardly slept at all.

In the morning Ramose stood in line to receive his breakfast. His stomach growled with hunger. He took his bread and dried fruit and was pleased to see that there was milk to drink. Just as he went to sit down with his food, one of the boys pushed him from behind and the food, milk and Ramose himself ended up in the sand. The tomb workers all laughed.

"That apprentice of yours has got two left feet, Paneb."

Ramose hated them all. He wanted to make them all suffer the same as he was, but he knew anything he said or did would only make them laugh at him more. He swallowed his anger and picked up the remains of his meal.

The job of an apprentice scribe was to keep a register of all the workers reporting for work every morning. If someone was late, he recorded it. If someone didn't come, he had to find out if they had a good excuse, such as being sick or having a special family feast day. He recorded that too. Then he had to note down all the tools they took from the store, all the pigment used to make paint, all the oil and wicks for the lamps. Even the water was rationed. The nearest water was the Nile and it had to be carried up by donkey from the river in big jars. Each man was only allowed six cups a day to drink.

Ramose collected the worn and broken chisels and took them back to the storeman. Copper was expensive and the chisels would be melted down and made into new chisels. At least once a day, Ramose dropped one of the stone flakes that he was writing on and had to pick up the pieces and fit them together again before he could copy the writing onto a fresh flake. He also had to walk up and down the steep stone ramp to the tomb again and again. Sometimes it was to fetch things from the store; sometimes it was to fetch a cup of water for Paneb. Paneb didn't do much at all.

The pace of work at the tomb was leisurely. Pharaoh was in good health and expected to live for another five or ten years at least. No one was in a great hurry to finish the work.

At meal times and in the evenings, the three boys did their best to make Ramose's life a misery. They never spoke to him, but from what they said to each other he got to know each of them. Nakhtamun was a short, stocky boy with a squashed nose and a shaved head. He was an apprentice sculptor. Hapu was an apprentice painter. He was quieter than the other two and always had a worried look as if he was sure he was going to get into trouble at any minute. Weni was the ringleader of the little group.

Weni was angry. It was he who had made Ramose drop the chisels. He was the boy who

was going to be apprentice scribe before Ramose came along. Now he was just a general errand boy at the tomb. Eventually he would have to leave and join the army or work in the fields. He was a sullen boy with a down-turned mouth, hard eyes and a scar on his cheek from a fight he once had with a sculptor wielding a chisel. Weni never smiled. Even when he won at senet he just scowled triumphantly at his opponents. The other two boys did whatever Weni said. The three boys hated Ramose. They wanted to get rid of him so that Weni could take his place.

Ramose tried to tell Samut, the foreman, about his problems with the boys, but the man wasn't interested.

"Sort out your own problems," he said. "Don't come telling tales to me."

This seemed most unjust to Ramose until he later found out that the foreman was Weni's uncle.

At the end of the eight-day shift, Ramose left the Great Place with relief. He didn't know if he had the strength to go back there again. The scribe's house now seemed large and bright. He collapsed onto the rickety bed which seemed unbelievably comfortable. His legs ached so much, he thought he might never get up again.

The next day, Ramose felt better after his first

full night's sleep in eight days. He had something important to do. After breakfast, he told the scribe he was going out for a walk.

"You're not going to try to run away again are you?" asked Karoya who was out in the garden grinding grain as usual.

"I don't have to tell you what I'm doing," snapped Ramose.

He walked briskly up the path that led towards the city, despite his sore legs. He wasn't running away though.

At the top of the hill he left the path and took ten measured paces to the north and then five to the east. There was a rock formation that looked a little like a lion ready to pounce. Ramose walked around it.

At the base, just where the lion's back paw would have been, there was a hollow. Ramose reached inside the hollow. Something was in there. He pulled out a small papyrus scroll. Ramose held the papyrus to his chest and smiled. It was a letter from Keneben. The tutor had arranged to leave a note for him after every shift at the tomb. Ramose broke open the seal and read the note eagerly.

The tutor Keneben greets his young lord, in life, prosperity and health and in the favour of Amun, King of the Gods, as well as Thoth, Lord of

God's words. May they give you favour, love and
cleverness whatever you do. How are you,
my lord? I am well as is your nanny, Heria. We
are both well. Tomorrow is in Ra's hands. We
work at our common goal and matters go well.
Your royal sister, Hatshepsut, has good health.
Write a note to us so that our hearts may be
happy.

The note told Ramose nothing really, but it made
him feel like singing. He read the letter again and
again, running his hands over the rough surface
of the papyrus and smelling its musky fragrance.
He pictured Keneben in the palace schoolroom
teaching Hatshepsut.

He then pulled out a stone flake from his bag.
He took out his palette and reed pens, as well as
a small jar of water. He sat cross-legged with his
back against the lion rock, dipped a pen in the
water, rubbed it on the ink block and wrote a note
back to his friends.

He thought of complaining about the miserable
life he had, the awful food, the rickety bed and
how everyone treated him badly. In the end
though, he didn't complain. He didn't want Heria
worrying about him. Instead he wrote that he had
seen his father's tomb, that he missed them both
and that he was counting the days until he could
see their faces again.

He let the ink dry in the sun and then he put the stone flake into the hollow for Keneben to collect.

Once or twice he thought he heard noises and wondered if someone had followed him, but it was just the sounds of rocks cracking in the heat or shifting with the wind. He looked towards the Nile and imagined he could smell the fertile smells of the river valley and see the white walls of the palace. Then he turned and went back to the village.

A LAPIS LAZULI HEART

THE NEXT SHIFT was not much different to the previous one, with one exception—this time Weni spoke to him.

Weni was unpacking food that had been sent up from the city on donkeys. Ramose was sitting out in his wedge of shade just outside the tomb entrance. He was transferring all his notes about the tomb workers' attendance from a dozen small

stone chips onto one large stone flake the size of a serving platter. He carefully copied down his notes for each day and totalled them up. Paneb would then recopy the details onto a papyrus scroll to be sent to the vizier at the end of the month.

Ramose sat back and looked at his work. Keneben would have been proud of him. His writing was in almost straight lines, apart from where the irregular stone surface went up and down. He smiled to himself and put it on the ground to dry in the sun. That's when Weni came up to him.

"Why don't you just go back where you came from?" Weni spat the words with hatred. "No one wants you here."

"I wouldn't be here if I didn't have to be," Ramose replied.

Weni was on his way down into the tomb with a water jar for the workers.

"You take this down, I don't feel like doing it," Weni said holding out the clay jar. The scar on his face and his small, hard eyes gave him a cruel look.

"Take it yourself," said Ramose.

A malicious look flashed into Weni's eyes. He tipped the jar sideways and water spilled all over Ramose's stone flake. His carefully written words quickly dissolved into grey swirls in the water,

and washed off the stone. Ramose watched as his work soaked into the sand.

"Look what you've done!" he shouted. "That took me nearly half a day."

"Serves you right," replied Weni. His mouth was twisted unpleasantly. It was the closest Ramose had seen him get to smiling. "You should have done as you were told."

Ramose stared at the blank stone flake. All his hard work was washed away. A few weeks ago that would have made him fly into a rage. Since he'd been in the Great Place his anger had been replaced by despair. He was powerless and alone there. Anger was pointless.

Ramose had to write his notes again after the workday was finished. Weni and the other boys wouldn't let him work in the hut. They suddenly needed an early night and complained when he lit a lamp. He went outside, looking for a place where his light wouldn't be seen. Inside the mouth of the tomb was the perfect spot. Ramose asked the night guard and he didn't seem to mind. It took him several hours.

When he had finished, Ramose didn't want to risk leaving it in his own hut in case one of the other boys got hold of it. Instead he carried it carefully to the scribe's hut. It was a moonless night and Ramose was scared he would trip and drop the stone flake and ruin his work again.

He entered Paneb's hut, ready to apologise for waking the scribe, but he was snoring deeply and didn't hear him. Ramose was tired but somehow not sleepy. He sat outside and looked up at the stars. He preferred the desert at night.

Ramose went to see Paneb before breakfast. He thought the scribe might be pleased with his work. He wasn't. Instead he grumbled about the lamp oil Ramose had used during the night.

"It has been reported to the foreman," complained Paneb. "You'll have to pay for the extra oil out of your wages."

Ramose sighed. It was stupid of him to think he could please the scribe. Paneb would never be happy. What did it matter? Ramose reminded himself that he was Pharaoh's son. One day he would be pharaoh. One day the workers who laughed at him, the boys who made his life so miserable, the grumpy scribe, they would all be working on his tomb. He would personally inspect their work. He would instruct them to make sculptures of the time he went into hiding in the Great Place. The pictures would tell the story of how he worked like a common man in order to foil the plans of his enemies at the palace. The tomb makers would remember how they had treated him and would beg their pharaoh's forgiveness. Ramose was looking forward to that day.

In the meantime, he had one more day in his current shift. He couldn't wait for the two days rest. Most of all he was looking forward to getting another letter from Keneben. He knew that if he could survive two shifts at the Great Place he could survive eighteen. That would be the end of the six months. Then his tutor and dear Heria would have prepared everything for his return to the palace. He found a small stone flake and made eighteen marks on it. He crossed one off. At the end of the day he would be able to cross off another.

That evening as he walked back to the tomb makers' village, Ramose felt good for the first time in a long while—since before Topi died. Nothing could spoil his good mood, not Paneb's grumbling, Weni's snide remarks or the sculptors' taunts.

When he got to the scribe's house, he greeted Ianna cheerfully and ran up the stairs to the roof so that he could get his clean kilt. When he got to the top of the stairs he stopped dead. Karoya was sitting on his bed with her arms folded. Spread out on the bed beside her were the contents of his chest.

"I told you not to touch my things," said Ramose angrily. "If you've stolen anything—"

"Who are you?" Karoya asked calmly.

"You know who I am."

"I know that you have a fine set of scribe's tools inlaid with ivory and jewels, yet you use the plain, old worn tools given to you by scribe Paneb." She picked up the gold rings. "And this gold must be worth a year's food rations for a whole family."

"I don't have to explain my possessions to a barbarian slave!" Ramose was trying to sound calm, but he wasn't.

"I've always felt there was something curious about you. When you first came, you hardly even knew how to tie your own kilt. And no orphan boy is used to drinking gazelle's milk. I want to know who you are."

Ramose snatched back the gold rings and wrapped them up again.

"And there's another thing about you," said the girl.

"What?"

"You are very rude. Egyptians are strange people, but they are polite. They always say thank you, even to a slave girl. You never do."

"If you tell anyone about this, I'll..." He could not think of anything to do to Karoya.

He needed time to think. He ran out of the house, out of the village and didn't stop till he got to the lion rock, his chest heaving, his breath rasping. He thrust his hand into the hollow. He had an awful feeling there would be no message for him, but his groping hand found not only a roll

of parchment, but also a knotted linen parcel. He
pulled them out with relief, broke the seal on the
papyrus and read the message.

*My prince, my heart is in mourning, I am
crouched with my head on my knees. The news
I have will bring you nothing but grief. Heria,
your beloved nanny, is resting from life.
She did not suffer but died peacefully in her
sleep. There is other news, less sorrowful but
still unwelcome. The queen has been in your
father's ear. She has appointed a new tutor for
her son, Prince Tuthmosis. I have been posted
abroad to the land of Punt. I have said farewell
to the Princess Hatshepsut. By the time you read
this letter, I will have left. Your secret is safe still.
I do not know when I will be able to contact you
again. My prayers will be with you every day.*

Ramose's shaking hands untied the linen bundle.
Inside was a beautiful blue jewel, almost too big
to fit into his hand. It was made from lapis lazuli
and shaped like a large beetle. It was edged in
gold and had two red garnets set in the stone
for eyes. On the beetle's back were carved the
three hieroglyphs that made up Ramose's name.
He turned over the jewel. The flat bottom was
covered with more hieroglyphs, tiny and finely
carved. It was his heart scarab, made to be buried

with his mummified body, wrapped tightly next to his heart. There was another scribbled note with it. It told briefly how Heria had managed to take this heart scarab from the dead body of the village boy. She had replaced the scarab with a ceramic one with the boy's own name on it. Hopefully the priests would not notice. Ramose looked at the scarab. It was so bright and so beautiful out there in the bleak, colourless desert.

Ramose sank down on his knees in the sand. In the last weeks he had held back his sadness, he had buried his loneliness, he had hidden his fears. Now he couldn't hold it in any longer. He had believed that his two friends would save him, now they were both gone. Heria, the nanny who had cared for him all his life, was lost to him forever. Keneben, his tutor, was far away in a foreign land. His father believed he was dead, and so did his beloved sister. The queen who hated him was still in the palace, still the pharaoh's favourite. He was alone in the world. Tears dropped one by one into the sand and disappeared, sucked into its dryness. Ramose wept and wept until the sand beneath his face was wet.

A hand touched his shoulder. Ramose looked up, startled. His first thought was that the palace guards had been sent to get him. It was Karoya.

"What's wrong, Ramose?" she asked.

Ramose wiped his face on his kilt.

"Why does the writing sadden you so?"

Karoya stroked his arm gently, just like Heria used to do when he was upset. She looked at him with what seemed like real concern. Then she suddenly stopped stroking. She was staring at the scarab in Ramose's hand.

"Where did you get that? I've never seen such a jewel."

Ramose sat back with the scarab in his lap, but said nothing.

"What sort of an apprentice scribe has such a thing and two handfuls of gold and scribe's equipment fit for a king?"

Ramose said nothing.

"Who are you?" asked Karoya peering at Ramose.

"You ask a lot of questions," he said.

Ramose felt that he had nothing more to lose. He needed to know that there was at least one person in Egypt who knew who he was and why he was in hiding.

"I am Prince Ramose," he said, trying his best to sound royal even though his face was streaked with dirt and tears. "Third son of the pharaoh. Heir to the throne of Egypt."

"The prince is dead. Even I know that."

"He's not dead. I'm not dead."

Karoya looked at the scarab, then at Ramose.

"Do you believe me?"

"That would explain a lot of your strangeness. Why would a prince be hiding in the village?"

Ramose told her the whole story, all about the deaths of his brothers, the evil queen, and his friends' fears for his life.

"My friends were supposed to be collecting evidence against the queen and the vizier, to convince the pharaoh that they had murdered my brothers and tried to murder me. Now my friends are gone there is no one in the world I can trust, apart from my sister, Hatshepsut, and she thinks I'm dead."

"You can trust me," said the slave girl. "I won't tell anybody."

Ramose looked at her and believed her.

"Thank you."

CARVED
IN STONE

KAROYA HAD kept her word and told no one what she had learned about Ramose. "Why do you have a jewel that is shaped like a beetle?" she asked as she kneaded bread dough in a large clay bowl.

"It's a heart scarab," replied Ramose who was sitting in the kitchen garden watching her.

"What's it for?"

"It's made to be buried with me when I die."

"It's very beautiful. It seems a shame to bury it in a tomb."

"When an Egyptian dies, their body is preserved so that it can travel into the afterlife."

Karoya glanced at him dubiously and started to shape the dough into flat round loaves.

"I've heard about this. They take out all the insides and wrap the body in strips of cloth."

"Not all of the insides—the heart is left in. In the afterlife Osiris, the god of the underworld, judges whether the person is fit to enter. Anubis, the jackal-headed god, takes the heart and weighs it against the feather of truth. If the heart exactly balances the weight of the feather, then Anubis knows the owner of the heart has been a good and truthful person and allows him to enter the afterlife."

Karoya fanned the small fire under the conical oven and added dry reeds and pats of animal dung to the flames.

"What happens if it doesn't balance?"

"Then the person is not fit for the afterlife. There is a monster called Ammut with the head of a crocodile, the front legs of a lion and the rear of a hippopotamus."

Karoya stopped fanning the fire.

"The monster comes and eats the heart of the bad person."

"And the beetle-shaped jewel?"

"It has my name on it. So that Osiris knows it is truly my heart. On the bottom of the scarab there is a prayer that no one will speak against me on that day of judgment."

Karoya took the rounds of dough and stuck them on the outside of the conical oven.

"Have you been a good person?" She didn't look him in the eyes as she usually did when she spoke to him.

Ramose had never really considered whether he was a good person or not. Would Osiris really question the goodness of Pharaoh's son?

"I'm not dead yet. When I am older, I will be pharaoh and I'll be a good pharaoh like my father. I'll treat my people well."

"And kill and enslave all foreigners," added Karoya.

The air was fragrant with the smell of baking bread.

"Maybe not."

The first loaf, now cooked, dropped to the ground.

"What are you going to do now?" Karoya asked quietly.

It was something Ramose had tried to avoid thinking about. The truth was he had no idea what to do.

"You only have two choices, as I see it," said

Karoya picking up the hot bread with the tips of her fingers. "You stay here and work in the Great Place or you go back to the city and let your father and sister know you are alive."

Ramose watched the other loaves fall from the oven one by one as they cooked. The thought of seeing his sister again lifted his heart.

"I have to go to the palace," he said after a while. "There's nothing else I can do." It felt good to make a decision. "I'll stay here until my father returns from his campaign."

Karoya picked up the other loaves and wrapped them in a cloth.

Ramose had begun to think that there was nothing he could do but stay forever in the Great Place counting chisels and recording absent workers. He'd imagined himself eating gritty bread and hearing people laughing at his clumsiness and making jokes about his fear of enclosed places till he was old and fat like Paneb. Talking to Karoya had helped him work out what he had to do. All he needed now was a plan, a way to get back into the palace.

In the meantime he would stay where he was and wait till his father returned from Kush. He had to work another shift at the Great Place.

Ramose decided to keep away from the other boys as much as he could. He would concentrate on the

work he had to do and try and stay out of trouble. He found a quiet spot behind the storehouse and started working on a stone flake. He was writing out a list of the provisions that had arrived from the city: sacks of grain, piles of smelly fish, several oxen ready to be slaughtered and fresh vegetables too. All of this had to be allocated to the workers according to their roles in the tombs.

They were paid once a month. The scribe and the foreman earned the most, seven or eight sacks of grain, then came the sculptors and painters, who earned six sacks. The labourers who hauled blocks of stone and baskets of stone chips each got four and a half sacks. Finally came the apprentices who earned two sacks of grain each. The perishable food was divided up more or less equally among the workers. Ramose wrote down his own earnings: two sacks of grain, a dozen fish, one and a half deben of oxen meat, a jar of oil and a basket of vegetables.

Ramose wouldn't be seeing any of his earnings though. He had to pay for the three copper chisels he'd damaged and the oil he'd wasted staying up half the night rewriting. He also had to repay Paneb for his scribe's tools and for feeding him while he had no income. It would be several months before he would actually get any payment himself.

Ramose's concentration was broken. He could feel someone watching him. He looked up. It was Karoya.

"What are you doing up here?" he said. "Why aren't you back in the village?"

"I have to fillet and salt the fish," she said. "It has to be dried before it can be given out to the workers."

"So will you be staying here in the Great Place?"

"For a few days. I go where I am told."

"It will be a change to have a friend here," Ramose said. "Ever since I arrived, all I've done is make enemies."

Samut came over. "Get back to your work, slave girl," he shouted at Karoya and raised his hand to hit her.

"I told her to come over here," said Ramose. "I need to record how many fish she has gutted."

Samut walked away grumbling. Karoya smiled at Ramose and went back to her work.

Now that he was used to the work and the walking up and down the tomb ramp every day, Ramose wasn't ready to fall into bed as soon as his day's work was over. He was bored. In the evenings, the workers sat around in small groups talking. Some worked on private sculptures either for their own tombs or to sell to others. They made small statues

of the gods or stelae, inscribed stones telling the gods all about the good things they had done in life. The painters sometimes brought up stools or small chests that they had made in the village. They painted them in their spare time and would sell them when they got home. The other boys often spent the evening playing games, but lately Weni had been working on a chest.

Ramose came back from the tomb carrying some stone flakes he wanted to check over before the sun set. Weni was sitting outside the hut carefully painting texts on the side of his chest in neat hieroglyphs. Ramose wasn't looking where he was going. He stumbled on a rock, staggered sideways to stop himself from falling over, and stood on Weni's chest. It was made of soft tamarisk wood, not hard imported wood. The chest splintered to pieces.

Weni was furious. His face turned red and he shouted angrily at Ramose, calling him every name he could think of.

"I'm sorry, Weni," said Ramose. "I didn't mean it. Truly."

"What difference does it make whether you meant it or not?" shouted Weni. "It's ruined anyway. Do you think I care whether you're sorry or not?"

After that incident Ramose decided to keep away from the hut until it got dark. He went

for a long walk. He climbed the hills behind the
Great Place. Not that there was anything to see.
In those bare hills the most exciting thing that
Ramose came across was a tuft of dry grass or a
lizard slithering under a rock or a scorpion boldly
warming itself in the lowering rays of the sun.
Walking gave him time to think.

Ramose knew that when he went back to the
palace, his problems wouldn't all be over. His
father would welcome and protect him, he could
be sure of that. His sister would rejoice that he
was still alive, he was certain of that as well.
Queen Mutnofret and Vizier Wersu would pretend
they were pleased that he was well, but secretly
they would still be plotting his death. He might
not survive there for long.

He was getting used to the idea that he might
die, but he hated the thought that his story would
never be known. One evening after the day's work
was over, Ramose decided to go for a walk up the
mountain which rose up from the valley on the
western side.

The peak of the mountain formed a natural
pyramid shape. It was a sacred place known as
the Gate of Heaven, which reached up to the sky
and the realm of the gods. It was the home of the
cobra goddess, Meretseger.

There were no paths leading up there. No one

ever climbed the Gate of Heaven, they had no
reason to.

Ramose picked his way through the rocks and
watched the workers' huts shrink and disappear
into the sand as he climbed. He climbed up
around the cliffs that surrounded the valley until
he was higher than the rim of the Great Place. He
could see over into the valley of the tomb makers'
village and beyond that to the Nile Valley. If he
squinted his eyes he could see a glint of white
from the temples on the eastern bank of the river.
He thought he might have seen a flash of gold
from a flagpole. It was probably his imagination
though. What he definitely could see was the sun
getting lower in the sky. He would have to hurry.

After the suffocating tomb and the cramped
and crowded hut, it was good to be alone and with
space around him to breathe. He kept climbing. A
vulture described slow, lazy circles above him. He
came to a second cliff face. There was an untidy
pile of twigs and dried grass perched on the top
of it. It was the vulture's nest. He looked up at
the great bird, symbol of the goddess Nekhbet,
protector of the pharaoh. The bird must have
flown many miles to bring the materials for its
nest to this desert place. It was a good omen. He
decided the place would suit his purposes well.

He unslung his reed bag and pulled out a copper
chisel and a stone flake covered in his own untidy

writing. He selected an area of the rock face, one that was set back in a fold of the cliff. For most of the day it would be in the narrow band of shade cast by the surrounding cliffs. At that time though, the rays of the setting sun shone onto it, burnishing it with an orange glow.

Before he set to work, Ramose said a short prayer to Thoth, the god of writing, and sprayed some drops of water on the cliff face. The text on the stone flake was the brief story of his escape from the palace. Now he was going to transcribe it onto the rock face. He got out his palette and a reed pen. First he marked vertical charcoal lines to help him keep the columns straight. Then, holding the stone flake in his left hand, he copied out the text in hieroglyphs. He wrote the words carefully in ink first.

In the eleventh year of the Pharaoh Tuthmosis, the first month of the season of peret, day seventeen, Prince Ramose, son of Pharaoh Tuthmosis and Queen Ahmose, beloved brother of Hatshepsut, lives. His enemies tried to end his life, but failed. Soon he will avenge their evil deeds. When his great father flies to heaven, Ramose will take his place as Pharaoh of Egypt.

The sun was getting low. Ra was about to start his perilous journey through the underworld

again. Before the sun rose again, the sun-god would have to defeat the serpent-god, Apophis. Ramose had to stop his work and get back to the valley. He scrambled down the cliffs in the gathering dark.

The next evening he returned and started to carefully chisel out the hieroglyphs. He had little experience at carving and it was slow work. He wanted it to be neat. He carved each hieroglyph with care. The work made him feel good. If Vizier Wersu and Queen Mutnofret succeeded and killed him, his story would be marked in stone forever. Somewhere in the world the truth would be written. Even if it was in a hidden fold of a cliff, high in the hills, deep in the desert where no one would ever see it.

He was concentrating hard, carving the first column of hieroglyphs.

"Why do you come all the way up here to write?" said a voice behind him.

Ramose nearly jumped out of his skin.

"Why do you go off climbing mountains in the desert by yourself?"

"I wish you wouldn't follow me everywhere," he said. It was Karoya, of course.

"Other Egyptians are afraid of the desert and huddle together in their huts. You go marching out into it alone."

"I don't like the desert any more than any other Egyptian. But I have a reason to be here."

Karoya looked at the hieroglyphs that Ramose had carved on the rock face.

"You could have carved pictures on rocks down in the valley."

"They aren't pictures. It's writing, the sort of writing used in the tombs. And I'm doing it up here because I don't want anyone to see it."

"What does it say?"

"It tells my story. If I die and never become pharaoh, it will be written here that I was betrayed."

"But no one will see it."

"Karoya, will you be quiet and let me work."

It took Ramose five visits to the cliff face to finish his carving. When he had carved the last hieroglyph, he washed off the ink and the charcoal markings and stood back to examine his work critically. He checked the hieroglyphs against his original writing on the stone flake to make sure he hadn't made any mistakes. Keneben would be proud of him, he thought. The hieroglyphs were well formed and even. The columns were straight. Perhaps even Paneb might have had a good word to say about his work.

It was getting late. The sun was about to sink below the horizon beyond the city. He hadn't

stayed on the mountain so late before. Ramose picked up his tools and packed them into his reed bag. He heard a sound behind him, a movement of stones. He turned.

"Is that you, Karoya?" he said. "I told you not to follow me."

A figure came out of the growing shadows, and another. It wasn't Karoya who had followed him. A third figure emerged. It was Weni and his friends.

"What are you doing up here, scribbler?" asked Weni.

"I don't have to tell you why I do things."

"Why have you brought your scribe's tools up here?" Nakhtamun was looking around.

"What I do is none of your business."

"What's this?" said Hapu. He was stooping to pick up the stone flake.

"It's mine," Ramose grabbed at the stone flake and hurled it down into the valley. He could see it smash into pieces as it bounced down the rocky hill.

Weni moved closer to Ramose, looking around suspiciously. He scanned the ground and then the cliff face, now brilliant orange in the last rays of the sun. Another step and he would see the carving. Ramose stepped in front of him.

"Get out of the way," Weni snapped and pushed Ramose aside.

Ramose was still not used to being touched by people. He was suddenly the spoiled prince again, furious that a common labourer had dared to touch him. He flung out his hand in anger to stop Weni from touching him again. The back of his hand caught Weni in the face. His knuckles struck Weni's nose. Ramose turned to see Weni with his hand to his face and blood pouring between his fingers.

Now it was Weni's turn to be furious. Weni hated losing. He pushed Ramose again, harder. Ramose fell backwards, sprawled in the dust. Ramose leapt to his feet and launched himself at Weni. He grabbed him by the hair and kicked him in the shins. The two boys wrestled to the ground. There wasn't much room to move. Nakhtamun urged Weni on.

"Hit him. He deserves it!"

Ramose broke free from Weni's grip and got to his feet again.

"Be careful," cried Hapu. "You're near the edge."

All the anger that Ramose had kept under control for the past weeks burst forth. He threw himself at Weni, punching and kicking him. The boys wrestled to the ground, rolling dangerously close to the edge. Stones rattled down the hill into the growing darkness below. Weni got to his feet again. Ramose lunged at him. Weni hit

out blindly in response. Ramose took a step back to avoid the blow. The ground beneath his foot crumbled and gave way. Ramose lost his balance and fell backwards. For a brief moment he saw the stunned faces of his three enemies staring down at him as he tumbled down the slope towards the cliff edge. He thought he saw a glint of triumph in Weni's eyes. Then their faces faded into darkness.

THE DESERT
AT NIGHT

RAMOSE AWOKE and shivered. He hoped it was a dream, but he was too scared to open his eyes. What if it wasn't? He opened one eye. It was dark. Ramose's body hurt. It hurt all over. His chest hurt most. His chest and his head. He could hear the scuffles of small creatures. He opened the other eye. He could see nothing but black. The goddess Meretseger's name meant

"she who loves silence". She punished people who disturbed her peace by making them blind. Had the fight with Weni offended the cobra-goddess? He moved his head a fraction to the left. The black was now dotted with tiny pin points of light. The stars. The souls of the dead. He wasn't blind. He was cold though. The desert at night was very cold. Ramose had never felt so cold in his life. Something with a lot of legs walked slowly over his arm.

This was the third time he'd woken up and thought that he might be dead. This time he was pretty sure he wasn't. There were rocks sticking into his back. His right arm was up against earth. He reached out and could feel the rough rocky surface sloping up above him. He carefully moved his left hand. There was rock under his elbow, but further out he could feel nothing but cold air. He was on a ledge. Whether he was one cubit off the ground or a thousand, he had no way of telling. He was too scared to move. The ledge was narrow and he didn't want to fall again. He didn't think he could sit up anyway.

No one would come looking for him until morning and even then they might not bother. Would they take the workers away from building Pharaoh's tomb just to look for an apprentice scribe who had bad handwriting and a fear of enclosed spaces? He doubted that they would. He

might be alive, but he didn't know for how long.

The moon slowly appeared above the starless black to his right. It was nearly full. With its light, Ramose could now see the shape of the rocky slope that he'd fallen down. The steeper cliff was below him. Ramose felt strangely at peace. Now that he was truly facing death he didn't feel afraid. He heard a howling in the distance. Hyenas. His heart suddenly leapt. His heart scarab was still in his reed bag up in the fold of cliff where he'd carved his story. When he reached the afterlife, how would Osiris know who he was? If the tomb makers buried him, the god of the underworld would think he was just an orphaned apprentice scribe. He would spend eternity as an apprentice scribe with no family.

A wave of loneliness washed over him. He wished he'd had a chance to see Hatshepsut again before he died. He had felt sad and lonely many times since that day in the palace when his pet monkey had died. If the truth was known, he was lonely even before then. But now he was completely alone. He was out in the desert, the land of the dead, far from the land of the living that clung to the Nile. A worse thought occurred to him. If no one found his body, he wouldn't go to the afterlife at all. His body would be eaten by vultures and hyenas. Then he would spend forever in oblivion.

Karoya might tell the tomb makers who he really was. They wouldn't believe her of course. She could take them to the carving he had made high in the cliffs of the Gate of Heaven. She might find his heart scarab so that it could be buried with him. He would have laughed if his chest wasn't hurting so much. His eternal salvation depended on a nosey, barbarian slave girl.

He drifted off to sleep and dreamt uncomfortable dreams of being lost in the underworld where even Topi the monkey didn't recognise him. He awoke again and the stars had moved. The moon was high above him. He was so cold he couldn't even move his fingers. The howl of the hyenas seemed closer.

There was one star that was crossing the sky so fast he could see it moving. It had a strange motion for a star. It seemed to be weaving back and forth in the sky. It was growing brighter. It was moving towards him. Perhaps Osiris knew he was about to die and was coming to get him. Perhaps he hadn't been abandoned after all.

"Ramose," said a voice. "Ramose, are you alive?" It was a female voice. Perhaps it was the cobra-goddess Meretseger come to lead him back up the mountain to heaven.

"I don't know," replied Ramose.

"I think we can assume you are," said another voice, a boy's voice.

The star lowered down to his face. It was an oil lamp in a hand. It was Karoya's hand. Her face came into the circle of light which made her black skin shine like polished ebony.

"Are you all right?" Another face came into the light. It was Hapu, the apprentice painter.

"Of course he isn't all right," said Karoya impatiently as she inspected Ramose in the lamplight. "He's covered in bruises and he's got a bad cut on his forehead."

She handed the lamp to Hapu and gently felt along Ramose's arms and legs. She held his head and moved it slowly to one side and then the other. She placed her hands on his chest. Ramose cried out in pain.

"You have some broken bones here," she said.

"We can't carry him," said Hapu.

"We don't have to carry him," replied Karoya. "He can walk."

Getting up and walking seemed like the most impossible thing in the world. Karoya pulled a leather pouch from her belt. She held it to Ramose's mouth. He felt liquid trickle down his throat. It wasn't water, it was wine. Ramose felt his insides warm. Karoya pulled a small metal box from the folds of her belt. Inside was something with a strong smell.

"What's that?" asked Ramose.

"Ointment from Kush. I only have a little left."

She rubbed the salve into Ramose's arms and legs. His limbs tingled and he could move his toes and fingers again.

"Hapu, you get behind him. We have to get him to his feet."

Hapu didn't know where to grip him. "I don't want to hurt him," he said.

"Sometimes pain can't be avoided," replied Karoya. "You push, I'll pull."

Ramose was thinking he was quite comfortable where he was, when an unbearably sharp pain in his chest made him cry out. Next thing he knew, he was on his feet.

The sky was starting to lighten. Ramose could now see that he had landed on a narrow ledge not much more than a cubit wide. If he had fallen any further, he would certainly have fallen to his death. Hapu was trying not to look at the sheer drop beneath them. It was a long way down.

"Let's get off this ledge."

"Can you walk, Ramose?"

Ramose nodded. His legs moved slowly and clumsily as if they were made of stone.

"I have your bag, Ramose," said Karoya. "We found it up higher where you and Weni fought."

She took Ramose's hand and led him slowly along the ledge until they came to a wider area that opened out and sloped down to the valley floor. Ramose had lost one of his sandals and the

other one was broken. Hapu gave him his sandals to wear.

"I'm sorry we left you on the mountain," he said.

With Hapu supporting Ramose on one side and Karoya on the other, they made slow progress. Ramose learned that Weni and Nakhtamun had told no one about the incident on the mountain.

"I saw them follow you up the mountain," said Karoya. "Then I saw them return at nightfall without you."

She had confronted the boys, demanding to know what had happened. Weni and Nakhtamun wouldn't tell her, but Hapu had told her what had happened.

"Weni said we'd tell the foreman if you hadn't returned by daylight," Hapu told him. "I knew you could be dead by then."

They'd waited until the moon rose and then gone to look for him.

By the time they reached the safety of the valley floor it was daylight. Ra had survived his perilous night journey. So had Ramose.

PLACE OF
BEAUTY

RAMOSE SCREWED up his nose. "What's that?"
Karoya was pressing something soft, wet
and foul-smelling against the wound on
his head.

"It's meat."

"It smells awful."

"A wound on the head must be treated with a
poultice of fresh meat on the first day."

"It doesn't smell fresh."

"It's as fresh as there is in this place."

"Is this another of your remedies from Kush?"

"No, I learnt this from an Egyptian priest." Karoya bound the meat to Ramose's forehead with a strip of linen. "Tomorrow I will just use oxen fat and honey."

"That sounds almost as bad," grumbled Ramose. "When I hurt myself back at the palace, priests said prayers over me and the royal jewellers made amulets to hang around my neck and ward off evil spirits."

"No priests. Just a piece of ox flesh."

"What about the broken bones in my chest?"

"They will heal as long as you rest."

Ramose didn't get to rest for long. He was given two days to recover before he was called before a special tribunal. Weni, Nakhtamun and Hapu were also summoned. The tribunal consisted of Scribe Paneb, Samut the foreman and two senior tomb workers.

"Why were you boys climbing the sacred mountain?" asked Paneb.

"We saw Ramose going up there and we were worried that he might get lost," Weni lied.

"And then when we found him, he just attacked Weni. He punched him in the nose," said Nakhtamun.

"Is this true, Ramose?" asked the foreman.

"I didn't mean to hit him," Ramose replied. "I just meant to push him away."

"I was just protecting myself," said Weni, "and then Ramose's foot slipped and he fell."

Hapu didn't say anything.

"You have behaved irresponsibly," said Paneb.

"We are all here at the Great Place to prepare the tomb of the pharaoh, may he have long life and health," said the foreman. "You striplings are privileged to work in this place. You have been trusted with knowledge of the whereabouts of Pharaoh's tomb. Only we tomb workers know this. The Great Place and the Gate of Heaven are sacred places."

"You should be banished from the Great Place," said Paneb. "But with two tombs now under construction we need all the workers we can get."

It was agreed that each boy should receive ten blows and pay a fine of a week's grain ration. Ramose was exempted from the beating, as he was already covered with purple and yellow bruises.

"I think it would be a good idea to separate you boys for a while," said Samut. "Ramose and Hapu, you can go to the Place of Beauty. Report to the foreman there tomorrow morning."

The Place of Beauty was the valley to the south of the Great Place. It was meant for the

burial of other members of the royal family.
There were three tombs there. Two belonged to
Ramose's brothers, Wadzmose and Amenmose.
The entrances to those tombs were hidden so
that tomb robbers couldn't find them. Ramose
found himself at the entrance of the third tomb
in the Place of Beauty, which was still under construction. It was his own tomb.

Ramose had been so busy in the Great Place,
concerned with daily life, the possibility of death
and the sharpness of chisels, that he hadn't had
time to think about the preparations for his own
burial. The mood of the workers at this tomb was
completely different to that of the men working
on Pharaoh's tomb. Men were hurrying about.
There was a sense of urgency. The moment the
two boys arrived, the foreman put them to work.
He sent Hapu down into the tomb to help the
painters.

"I want you to check the script on the tomb
walls," the foreman told Ramose. "This has been
a rushed job and our scribe has been ill for weeks.
Check for mistakes."

Ramose entered the tomb and the cool air gave
him goose bumps. It was a small tomb compared
to his father's. A few steps led down to a short
corridor, which opened straight into the burial
chamber. The chamber was a strange shape.
Instead of being rectangular, it was narrow at one

end. One corner had an ugly, jagged lump sticking out of it. The foreman saw Ramose looking at it. "The quarry men ran into a flint boulder in the rock," he explained. The rock deep in the desert hills was generally quite soft and easy to carve, but occasionally there were outcrops of hard flint. The tomb makers' copper chisels buckled and broke when they hit flint.

"We didn't have time to start a new excavation, so we had to leave it. It'll make it difficult to fit the sarcophagus in, but it can't be helped."

Ramose looked at the artwork on the walls. A team of six painters, now including Hapu, were painting texts on three of the walls. They were instructions for how to travel through the dangerous underworld. The painters were also drawing maps showing two different ways to get past the monsters and lakes of fire. Hapu was on his knees, painting a border of papyrus reeds and Horus eyes.

"We've only had time to carve sculptures on one of the walls," said the foreman.

"Will there be no carvings in the corridor?

"No, there isn't time."

Ramose opened his mouth to complain.

"It's not my fault the royal princes keep dying so young," grumbled the foreman. "Three tombs in two years! How are we supposed to cope?"

Ramose looked closer at a half-finished carving

of Anubis, the jackal-headed god of the dead, leading a young boy into the presence of Osiris, the god of the underworld. A sculptor was gently chipping away at the rock to shape the boy's kilt. Another sculptor was carving the boy's name alongside in elegant hieroglyphs. It was Ramose's name.

Ramose realised that the carving was of himself. His heart was being weighed against the feather of truth. Thoth, the ibis-headed god of writing, was noting down the results. The monster Ammut, part crocodile, part lion, part hippopotamus watched, ready to pounce on the heart and devour it if it was heavy with wrong-doing.

Another sculptor was working on the other end of the wall. He was putting the finishing touches to a carving of Ramose's family: Pharaoh, his mother, his beautiful sister Hatshepsut, his two brothers and himself as a small boy. He was sitting on his mother's lap. A cat was playing under her chair.

It probably wasn't a real likeness of his mother. The man who had drawn the outline for the sculptor would never have seen her. Ramose couldn't remember what she looked like. He held a lamp up to the image of his mother's face. It was beautiful. Calm and smiling. One elegant hand was resting on the shoulder of the child on her lap. Another sculptor, who was working

on the hieroglyphs, had finished his work on the other carving. He came over and started to carve the names of the family members. He was a skilled craftsman. Following the outlines painted on the walls, he carved the shapes with smooth assured strokes. The hastily drawn outlines were transformed into neat three-dimensional hieroglyphs, each one a small work of art.

Ramose looked closer. Next to the image of his mother the sculptor had carved the hieroglyphs for Mutnofret.

"Stop!" Ramose reached out and grabbed hold of the sculptor's hand.

"What do you think you're doing, stripling?" said the sculptor.

"You've made a mistake," said Ramose angrily.

The sculptor turned to look at the new apprentice scribe, surprised by the tone of his voice. "What are you talking about?"

"Mutnofret is only a lesser queen. The name of the Great Royal Wife was Ahmose. You've carved the wrong name."

"We're in a hurry," the sculptor said, going back to his carving. "I haven't got time to redo it."

"You have to change it," shouted Ramose as he prised the chisel from the sculptor's hand.

Hapu looked over to see his new friend grappling with the sculptor. He ran across to restrain Ramose before he got hurt in the scuffle.

"Calm down, Ramose. Does it matter if it's the wrong queen?"

"Yes it does matter. It matters a lot. Mutnofret isn't the Prince Ramose's mother. It has to be changed."

Ramose stopped struggling and Hapu released his hold. As soon as he was free, Ramose lunged at the sculpture and with the chisel attacked the name of the hated queen. He gouged the first two hieroglyphs from the wall before the startled tomb workers realised what he was doing and wrestled him to the floor. Ramose fell hard and cried out in pain as his unhealed ribs hit the stone floor.

Hapu pushed through the knot of men around his friend and knelt at his side.

"He's still recovering from an accident," Hapu pointed to the gash on the side of Ramose's head. "He fell. It's affected his judgment a little."

"A lot, I'd say," said the sculptor looking at the damage done to his work.

The foreman came into the burial chamber.

"What's all the noise about?"

"This new apprentice scribe is gouging holes in the walls."

"It was wrong," said Ramose holding his chest. "I just wanted the queen's name to be right. You told me to check for mistakes."

"I didn't tell you to gouge holes anywhere."

The men looked at the apprentice scribe and

shook their heads as they went back to their work. Ramose took a stone flake and a pen from his bag. He wrote his mother's name on it as neatly as he could.

"This is the real queen's name," he said, handing it to the sculptor.

"Plaster over the damage," said the foreman, "and recarve the queen's name." He turned to Ramose. "You," he said angrily. "Go and check the painted hieroglyphs on the other walls, that's what you're here to do."

Ramose and Hapu ate their midday meal out in the valley. "You must like getting into trouble," Hapu said with a wry smile.

"Of course I don't."

"You wouldn't think so," said Hapu through a mouthful of dried fish. "We've only been here for one morning and you've already upset half the team and been fined a sack of grain for damaging the tomb."

Ramose dipped bread into his lentil soup, and ate it without commenting.

"You're a strange person." Hapu looked at Ramose, trying to work out his new friend.

"What's strange about me?"

"You climb mountains by yourself, you attack tomb carvings, you have a slave for a friend."

"I have good reasons for all of those things."

"I'm sure you do, but I don't know what they are."

"I can't explain."

"Perhaps it's because you come from the south."

"Maybe." Ramose was keen to change the topic of conversation. "Do you miss your friends?" he asked Hapu.

"Not much. Weni isn't really my friend. He's a troublemaker."

"Like me."

"No, not like you. Weni's mean. He likes to hurt people. You don't get into trouble on purpose." Hapu laughed. "You're not mean, you're just not very smart."

Ramose laughed too. A few weeks ago, if anyone had made fun of him in that way, he would have been angry. Now he didn't mind.

"Come on, you boys," said the foreman as he passed by them in a hurry. "Time to get back to work. A messenger just came up from the city. There's going to be a royal visit."

"The pharaoh?" asked Hapu. "He's coming here?"

"That's right, Pharaoh himself, may he have long life, health and prosperity. He'll be here in a few days to see how his tomb's progressing. Half our team will have to go down to the village to get his residence in shape."

"Will he be coming to inspect the prince's tomb as well?" asked Ramose.

"Yes, and we have orders to finish it before he does."

Ramose's heart started thudding. He didn't have to worry about how he could get into the palace to see his father. His father was coming to him. This was Ramose's chance. He could see his father and let him know that he was still alive.

ROYAL VISIT

THE TOMB WORKERS spent the next nine days working very long hours to get the tomb finished. There wasn't really enough time, but they did their best to have the tomb as close to finished as they could. Ramose was grateful to them for this, even though it wasn't him that was going to be buried there. He checked the texts on the walls carefully. The peasant boy who was to

be buried there in his place deserved to find his way safely through the underworld.

At the end of the shift there was a feast to celebrate the completion of the tomb and to thank the workers for their hard work. Extra food was released from the tomb stores and special bread and cakes were baked. There was to be a holiday as well. Instead of the usual two days break, the workers had four days before they had to report back to duty at the Great Place.

Ramose and Hapu walked wearily up the path. When they reached the top of the hill, they could see the village below them. Usually there was no sign of activity and the mud brick village could easily have been mistaken for part of the landscape. Now people were running around between the village and the dusty mud brick building which stood outside the village walls. The building had been half-finished the whole time Ramose had been in the valley.

In their absence, it had been hastily transformed into a royal residence. Its walls were now finished. The end wall had darker patches where the fresh mud bricks hadn't quite dried. The other walls were being whitewashed. Men were clearing rocks from around the building and levelling a path branching off from the one that came down the opposite hill from the city. Other men were erecting two gold-tipped flagpoles just like the

ones that circled the palace on the banks of the
Nile. A dozen donkeys stood outside the building.
People hurried back and forth unloading piles of
furniture and food from the donkeys' backs.
Karoya was waiting at the village gate for
them.

"You've heard the news I suppose?" she asked
as they approached.

"About Pharaoh's visit?" said Hapu. "Of course
we've heard. We had to get the prince's tomb
ready for inspection."

"The donkeys have been coming and going all
day. I've never seen such things. Look at that
furniture!"

Chairs and low tables were being carried into
the residence. Each item was painted in bright
colours or inlaid with gold and turquoise and
lapis lazuli. There were also three gold-painted
couches carved in the shape of animals: a lion, a
leopard, a gazelle.

Karoya looked at Ramose. He hadn't said a
word. She knew what this meant for him.

Hapu was chatting on, unaware. "We had a feast
in the Valley, with wine and sweet cakes," he said.
"Didn't you save a cake for Karoya, Ramose?"

Ramose nodded and pulled a linen package from
his bag and handed it to Karoya. She unwrapped
the present and smiled. It was a cake in the shape
of a cat.

"What will we do for four days?" Hapu asked as they walked into the village.

"I have a few ideas," said Ramose.

The next morning the scene outside the village hardly seemed to have changed. More donkeys were arriving laden with goods for the royal residence. Ramose and his friends were all called on to help with the work. Holiday or not, everyone had to make sure everything was ready for Pharaoh.

In the afternoon, ignoring the heat of the sun, the entire population of the village gathered outside to welcome their pharaoh. Few of them had ever seen him before. They waited and waited. Ramose stood nervously among the crowd. They waited some more.

"Why have you brought your palette and pen?" asked Hapu.

"I might be needed to record something," said Ramose vaguely.

Karoya guessed he had a plan, but she didn't know what it was.

Eventually a party of about twenty people on foot appeared over the rim of the valley.

"There are so many of them," said Karoya who was standing upon a rock so she could get a better view. "I wonder which one of them is Pharaoh?"

Hapu laughed.

"None of them. They're all servants, musicians, dancers, cooks."

Two covered chairs appeared on the path. They were draped with white cloth edged in gold and carried on poles by more servants.

"That's Pharaoh," said Hapu.

"But he's covered up. I won't be able to see him," said Karoya disappointed.

"You'll be in his presence, that's enough."

"Who is in the other covered box?" asked Karoya, craning her neck still hoping to get a glimpse.

"I don't know," said Ramose. "Probably Queen Mutnofret."

Ramose knew that if he was going to act, it had to be now. While his friends were peering at the royal procession, he moved towards the workers who were frantically carrying in the last of the food supplies. Four donkeys were still waiting patiently as they were unloaded. The gateway to the royal residence was guarded by two men armed with daggers. Ramose walked up to the donkeys and whacked one of them on the rump. The startled animal took off at great speed, trampling through a pile of vegetables. The other donkeys galloped after it.

"Quick," shouted Ramose to the guards. "Catch those animals. Pharaoh approaches. He'll be here in a matter of minutes."

The guards obediently ran after the donkeys.

Ramose pulled out his scribe's palette and a stone flake and pretended to jot down some notes. He picked up a basket of onions and walked in through the gate.

His plan was hazy. He didn't want to present himself to his father in a crowd of people. It would be a shock, after all his father thought he was dead. What he wanted to do was hide somewhere and go to his father when he was alone in his private chamber. The courtyard was a frenzy of last minute activity. Ramose strode through it and into the residence as if he belonged there. He did belong there.

People were rushing around inside as well. Ramose marched down the corridor purposefully, carrying his palette and with a reed pen pushed behind his ear. No one questioned him.

Two chambers had been prepared. One was full of women arranging mirrors, cosmetics and draperies around a bed. He glimpsed the golden animal-shaped couches. The chamber opposite had a larger bed with a carved wooden canopy and a beautiful gilt chair decorated with carved lions' heads and with winged serpents as armrests. Ramose entered the room. Light from the lowering sun slanted in through grilles in the ceiling and lit up the rich fabric on the bed. He sniffed the cool air, which was sweet with frankincense. Off the main room was a smaller room with a white

alabaster bath sunk into the floor. Large clay
water jars, almost as tall as Ramose, stood next
to the bath. The jars were full of fresh water to
pour over Pharaoh. It was Nile water carried all
the way up from the river valley.

The voices and running feet in the residence
suddenly fell silent. Ramose knew the royal
procession had arrived. He stayed in the bathing
room and waited. His heart was beating so loud
that it seemed to fill the silent room. He was
going to see his father. He only had to wait a few
minutes, but it seemed like a long, long time.
Then he heard a deep voice rasp out orders in the
outer chamber.

"Where is my clean clothing? Bring me some
wine at once."

The voice was familiar. It was a voice he'd
known all his life. But it wasn't his father's. It
was the impatient, angry voice of Vizier Wersu.

"I want to get out of these dirty clothes and
wash off the dust from this wretched place."

Ramose looked around. There was nowhere to
hide. He heard servants rush in with the vizier's
clothes chest. He heard footsteps approaching.
Ramose knew that if the vizier saw him he would
be dead before the end of day. He had no choice.
There was only one place to hide. Ramose hoisted
himself up and into one of the huge water jars. The
cold water took his breath away. As he lowered

his body into the jar, the water overflowed onto the white stone floor. The water level was right at the lip of the jar. Ramose's head was still in full view. The footsteps grew louder. Ramose closed his eyes and ducked his head under the water. With his head tipped back, he could just manage to hold his nose above the surface.

The vizier came into the room. From under the water, Ramose could hear the distorted sounds of his crocodile voice shouting at the servants. Even though there was two finger-widths of clay between them, Ramose felt exposed. He'd always had the feeling that Wersu could see through walls. He was terrified that the vizier would discover him. He closed his eyes.

All the time he'd been in the desert, Ramose had dreamt of immersing his body in the waters of the Nile, of feeling its coolness and smelling the humid air around it. This wasn't what he'd had in mind. He felt trapped. He tried to imagine that he was floating in the Nile instead. That he wasn't cramped in a water jar like a mummy in a coffin. He sucked long deep breaths of air through his nose to calm him. I am in the river, he told himself. I am drifting in the river among lotus flowers and fish. Hopefully the servants would use the other jar to get water to bathe the vizier.

Ramose could hear footsteps echoing hollowly outside the jar. A dull clunk of something banging

against the clay made him jump. He opened his eyes. A hand swam into view above him holding a large copper dipper. Ramose took a deep breath and pulled his head right under the water, crouching down inside the jar. The dipper plunged into the water above his head. It seemed to take an age for it to fill and then to be lifted out again. Finally it disappeared from sight. Ramose raised his head.

As his nose broke clear of the surface, in his hunger for air, he breathed in water. He spluttered and water filled his mouth and nose. He pushed his head right out of the jar alternately coughing and greedily gulping in air. Fortunately the vizier was facing away from the jar and loudly complaining about the lack of cleansing oils in this makeshift place. His servant was concentrating on pouring the water over the vizier's head. Neither of them heard or saw Ramose.

The dipper plunged in another ten or more times, and each time the water level fell until Ramose could crouch in the jar's depths with his head clear of the water.

When Vizier Wersu had finished bathing, Ramose waited until the outer chamber was silent again. He climbed out of the jar and dripped into the other room. He slumped down on the gilt chair with the lion head decorations and the winged serpent armrests. Now that he could breathe easy

again, he had time to feel bitter disappointment. His father wasn't in the inspection party. Only two rooms had been prepared, this one and the one opposite which was obviously arranged for a woman. He had thought that his ordeal was over, and it wasn't. His father was as far away as ever. His plan was ruined.

He heard more footsteps approaching, the crash of a dropped tray and angry muttered words. He didn't move. He didn't care if he was discovered in the vizier's rooms. A face peered around the doorway, a dark face framed by a twist of red and green material. It was Karoya. She slipped into the room noiselessly. There was another crash and Hapu stumbled into the room carrying a large copper platter of jumbled fruit.

"Your friend is as stealthy as an elephant," whispered Karoya angrily to Ramose. She glared at Hapu. "I told you not to follow me."

Hapu was not normally clumsy, but it was obvious from his face that he was very nervous. "We could be put to death for this," he said. "What are you doing here, Ramose?"

"It's a long story," sighed Ramose.

"Get up off that chair! You'll damage it, dripping on it like that. The gold paint will peel off."

Ramose took no notice of him.

"Pharaoh isn't here," said Karoya.

"I know."

There was despair in Ramose's voice.

"I don't understand why you came in here at all," said Hapu. "It's just as if you are looking for trouble."

"I'm not looking for trouble."

"Well let's get out of here then, before anyone comes."

Ramose didn't move. Karoya grabbed him by the arm.

"Come on, Ramose," she said.

She dragged Ramose to his feet and peered around the door frame. "There's no one around."

She crept out into the corridor still holding on to Ramose.

"Bring the tray," she ordered Hapu. "In case we run into anyone."

They had no sooner stepped through the doorway into the corridor than laughter could be heard from someone approaching. A group of women rounded the corner chattering and laughing. They were like a vision, all wearing flowing white gowns and jewellery. The smell of perfume filled the corridor. Karoya froze.

"Keep walking," whispered Hapu. "Don't look at them."

Karoya did as Hapu said, pulling Ramose behind her. They passed the laughing women with bowed heads and purposeful steps. One of the women spoke just as they passed them.

"I hope they brought some gazelle milk up from the valley," she said.

Ramose stopped dead and turned towards the woman.

"Hatshepsut!"

GIFTS FROM
A PRINCESS

"**W**HO CALLS Princess Hatshepsut's name?" demanded one of the women.

"Ramose, now what are you doing?" whispered Hapu unable to believe his friend was looking for more trouble. "What's wrong with you? We were almost out of here."

Ramose didn't hear either of them. He was

staring at his sister. It was only just over two months since Ramose had seen her, but she had changed in that short time. She had lost her girlishness and become a young woman. He felt a rush of jumbled emotions: love, pride, homesickness. Karoya stood with her mouth open, staring at the beautiful princess.

Hatshepsut had a dazzling white gown that fell from her waist in finely pressed pleats. Around her neck was a deep collar made of gold with thousands of semi-precious stone making up a wonderful design of lotus flowers. She had matching armbands and earrings. She was wearing a wig divided into hundreds of tiny plaits, each one ending in a gold bead in the shape of a cowry shell. On top of it was a gold crown with a rearing snake's head on it. Her eyes were lined with kohl and her eyelids painted a shimmering green. She looked like a goddess.

Hapu didn't know what to do in front of such a vision so he fell to his knees and bowed down before her. Ramose stood smiling at his sister, he reached out to make sure she was real. Hatshepsut pulled her arm away before he could touch her. Her four companions drew around their mistress as if she might be contaminated by closeness to such an inferior person.

"What is it that you want, servant?" asked Hatshepsut. Her voice was like music from a lute.

"Why are you in this part of the residence? Only my personal maids and the vizier's servants are permitted in here."

Karoya just kept staring. Hapu tried to speak but failed. Ramose's smile faded. He realised that his sister didn't know who he was.

"Penu," he said. "Don't you recognise me? It's Ramose."

Hatshepsut turned and studied his face.

"Ramose?" she said.

"Your brother."

The calm, self-confident look on the princess's face faded as she stared at the wet-haired boy in the stained kilt. She changed before his eyes from a composed princess to a confused young girl. She peered into his face.

"Ramose?"

"You've changed so much in such a short time. Have I changed too?"

Hatshepsut reached out and pushed a lock of wet hair back from his face and touched the scar on his forehead.

"Is it really you, Ramose?"

Ramose nodded. "It's me, Penu."

Hatshepsut put her arms around her brother. Ramose felt her wet cheek brush his as he hugged her. He wanted to cry out with happiness. He had his sister back.

In Hatshepsut's chamber, Ramose sat next to

her on the golden gazelle-shaped couch and told her his story. He told her about his faked death, his escape to the tomb makers' village and how the banishment of Keneben his tutor had cut off his only link with the palace. He told her how much he'd missed her. Hapu sat with his mouth open as he heard the story for the first time. Hatshepsut listened, her face pale with shock.

"You've been very brave," she said when he finished. "Father would be proud of you."

"I thought that Father was going to be in the inspection party," Ramose said.

"He isn't well. I took his place at the last minute." Hatshepsut's face clouded with sadness. "He became ill while he was in Kush." The princess glanced at Karoya.

"I have to see him," said Ramose. "I have to let him know that I'm still alive."

"I don't think it would be a good time to go back," said Hatshepsut. "Mutnofret is even more powerful now. She acts as if her brat is already pharaoh. She and Wersu are acting together as co-regents. Father is too ill to realise what she's doing."

"What do you want me to do? Stay here for-ever?"

"No, of course not," said Hatshepsut taking her brother's hand. "Just wait. Wait until father is strong again. I'll arrange for Keneben to be sent

back to Thebes. I'll send you word when it's safe to come, when Wersu and Mutnofret are away from the palace. It won't be long, I promise."

"I want to go home, Penu." Ramose felt tears well in his eyes. He couldn't help it. The memories of home flooded back.

Hatshepsut reached out and hugged him again.

"I can't imagine what it's been like for you, living as you have and being all alone."

"I haven't been alone," he said, turning to Karoya and Hapu.

As soon as the princess looked at Hapu, he fell to his knees again.

"This is Hapu," said Ramose. "He's an apprentice painter in the Great Place. We've been working together there on Father's tomb. He's become a good friend."

Hatshepsut smiled. "He seems rather stunned by these events."

"He's only just found out who I am."

He turned to Karoya. "And this is Karoya. She's a slave from Kush who grinds grain for the scribe."

"A slave? You have a strange collection of friends, Ramose."

"Karoya saved my life."

"The slave girl doesn't seem surprised to know who you are."

"I told her some time ago. She had already half guessed, anyway."

"A very clever slave it would seem."

"A very inquisitive slave," replied Ramose smiling at Karoya.

Hatshepsut had regained her composure. She looked and sounded like a princess again.

"Here," she said taking off one of her bracelets and handing it to Karoya. "A reward for taking care of my brother. I suspect he's needed some help."

"I don't need a reward," said Karoya looking the princess in the eye.

"Then take it as a gift from me."

Karoya took the bracelet from the princess, turning it over in her hands so that it caught the rays of sun that were angling in through the grilles in the ceiling.

Hatshepsut looked down at Hapu who was still on his knees.

"Stand up," she said touching him on the head.

Hapu stood up, blushing under the princess' gaze. "I'd like to thank you as well for helping my brother." She went over to a chest and opened the lid. It was full of jewellery.

Karoya stared at the chest. "I've never seen so much gold and jewels," she said.

"This is just my travelling chest," said Hatshepsut reaching into the chest.

She pulled out a small amulet on a gold chain. "Here," she said. "Take this. It's in the shape of the knot of Isis, so that the goddess will watch over you."

Hapu took the amulet in his hand. It was made of red jasper and finely carved with papyrus reeds. He opened his mouth to thank the princess, but his voice failed him again. Princess Hatshepsut smiled at the apprentice painter, aware of the effect she was having on him. She turned to Ramose.

"There is a banquet I must attend. Wersu will be wondering where I am."

Ramose glanced at the women. "Can we trust them?"

"Yes. They'll do whatever I ask them," said Hatshepsut. "I'll send one of them with you to the gate, so that I know you got away safely."

Ramose hugged his sister, clinging onto her, not wanting her to go. She pulled herself gently away. Ramose watched her as she swept out of the rooms. Part of him would have given anything to follow her and step back into his old life again. Another part of him knew he had to follow through what he'd started. He turned back to his friends.

"She's..." said Hapu. It was all he could manage to say.

Ramose smiled. "We'd better get out of here," he said. He led his friends down the corridor.

When they reached the courtyard, they were surprised to find it was almost dark. They were more surprised to find six royal guards barring their way with long-handled spears. A tall, thin figure in a long robe stepped out of the shadows. He was holding a lamp in insect-like hands. It was Vizier Wersu.

The lamplight threw sharp shadows on his crocodile face. Behind him were two smaller figures dressed in the working kilts of the tomb makers: Weni and Nakhtamun.

Ramose hung back in the shadows behind Karoya where the vizier couldn't see his face.

"Search them," ordered Wersu. Three guards stepped forward and grabbed Ramose and his friends.

"Take your hands off me," yelled Karoya punching the guard as he tried to search through the folds of her belt. He found the princess's bracelet and held it up.

The guard holding Hapu easily found the amulet that the princess had given him.

"See, I told you they'd come into the royal residence to steal," said Nakhtamun triumphantly.

"I can't find anything on this one, sir," said the guard searching Ramose. "Wait a minute, bring over the light."

The vizier strode over towards Ramose.

"He's got something in his hand."

The guard grabbed Ramose's hand and roughly prised open his fingers. In the palm of his hand was his heart scarab. The lamplight illuminated the blue and gold of the scarab and a trick of the light made it look huge.

"It's a heart scarab," said the vizier, moving his lamp closer to the jewel in Ramose's hand. "A royal one by the look of it."

"He's a tomb robber!" cried Weni. "I knew he was up to something."

Ramose turned his head away, afraid that the vizier would recognise him.

"He's not a tomb robber," cried Hapu. "You don't know who you've got there."

The vizier turned to Hapu.

"You'll be very sorry you did this, Weni," continued Hapu. "Ramose is no thief, he's—"

"Someone I summoned to the residence," said a calm voice behind them.

Everyone turned and saw Princess Hatshepsut drifting toward them in the light of four lamps held by her female companions. The circle of light only reached as far as her knees, giving the illusion that she was floating above the ground. The red eyes in the snake's head on her crown flashed.

"I thought it would be amusing to meet some people my own age who live and work out here in the desert," said Hatshepsut looking Vizier

Wersu square in the eye. "Why are you holding my guests at the point of a spear?"

"I have been informed that they are thieves," said the vizier. "The slave girl has what looks to be one of your bracelets, Highness."

"It was a gift from me, as was the amulet that I gave to the young man who blushes easily."

Hapu blushed again.

"What about the heart scarab? Surely that has been stolen from a tomb."

Ramose glanced at his sister. She wouldn't be able to explain away the scarab so easily. Her face was as calm as ever.

"Really, Vizier Wersu," said Hatshepsut with a laugh. "Can't you tell a real lapis lazuli scarab from the painted ceramic copies that can be bought at any market stall in the city?"

The vizier peered at the stone in the dim light. Ramose kept his head turned away and his heart scarab firmly in his hand.

"Now, Vizier," continued Hatshepsut. "If you've finished, I think you have kept the tomb officials waiting long enough. They are wondering where you are."

Vizier Wersu was angry at being made to look foolish. "I'll see that you boys receive ten lashes and a fine of a month's wages for this," he said glaring at Weni and Nakhtamun.

Hatshepsut turned and drifted serenely back

into the royal residence in the halo of light provided by her companions.

"Come along, Vizier," she said.

The vizier dismissed the guards with a jerk of his head and followed the princess. The guards escorted Weni and Nakhtamun out. Ramose watched his sister until she was out of sight. Hapu turned to Ramose.

"Why didn't you tell me you were a prince?" said Hapu. "Didn't you trust me to keep your secret?"

"It had nothing to do with trust," said Ramose. "It's dangerous knowledge. I didn't want to put you at risk."

Hapu looked at his friend with confusion. "I don't know how to speak to you any more."

"Speak to him the same as you always have," exclaimed Karoya. "He's the same person he was when you thought he was an apprentice scribe."

Hapu didn't look convinced.

"She's right," said Ramose. "When I first came here I was a spoilt prince. I think I've changed."

"Oh," said Karoya, "and what are you now?"

Ramose thought for a moment. "I'm still a prince," he said. "But now I'm a prince who knows what it's like to get dirt under his fingernails."

Karoya laughed.

Ramose was standing on a dry, rocky hill. He looked around. There wasn't a blade of anything

growing. He looked down at himself. His clothes were dusty and his reed sandals were worn. He knew exactly where the remains of his red leather sandals were, the ones with the turned-up toes: they had been thrown into the rubbish pit outside the tomb makers' village weeks ago.

He heard a mournful chanting drifting up from below. Snaking along in the valley was a procession. At the front was a jackal-headed priest. The sun reflected on gold and jewels. A beautiful coffin on an ornate sled was being pulled by six oxen. Six priests followed behind. They all wore brilliant white robes with leopard skins draped over their shoulders. It was a funeral procession. Ramose looked closer. How many loads of funeral goods were there? How many mourners were there?

He had a special interest in this funeral.

It was his own.

It was just like his dream seventy days ago, except this time he knew for sure it wasn't a dream and he knew that he wasn't dead.

"Look!" he said to Hapu. "That's my funeral."

Hapu smiled awkwardly. He was still getting used to the fact that his friend was a prince. "It looks impressive. Nicely painted sleds and tomb furniture from what I can see."

Karoya was standing on his left, with the length of red and green cloth wrapped over her

head to shield her from the sun. The princess's
gift glinted on her arm. "A lot of fuss for a clumsy
apprentice scribe, I'd say."

Ramose smiled at his friends. That was why he
knew he wasn't dreaming. In his dream he'd been
alone and frightened in a strange place. Now he
knew where he was, he knew where he was going
and he had the company of friends.

He looked back over the desert hills to the
green Nile valley and the silver strip of the river.
Somewhere within the whitewashed walls beside
the river, below the pennants fluttering from gold-
tipped flagpoles, was his sister. That was where
his future lay, over there in the palace on the
banks of the beautiful river. But for now he had a
life over the next hill in the Great Place, another
shift to work. He turned back to the path.

A WORD FROM THE AUTHOR

THE HISTORY of the ancient Egyptians spans a period of three thousand years from around 3000 BC to 30 BC. They lived a long time ago, but we have lots of information about them. One reason for this is because of the tombs they built to preserve the bodies of pharaohs. The tombs contained all the everyday things they needed in the afterlife, such as furniture, cooking pots and clothing. The walls of the tombs were decorated with pictures of daily life. The tombs have been robbed or destroyed over the millennia, but there is still enough remaining to tell us a lot about the way Egyptians lived.

The other reason we know so much about ancient Egyptian life is that the Egyptians liked writing. They kept records of everything they did. Near the village of the tomb workers, in the area now known as the Valley of the Kings, archaeologists found a rubbish pit filled with thousands of stone chips, all covered with writing. From these chips we have learnt an amazing amount of detail about the lives of these ordinary people: what they ate, what they were paid, arguments they had with each other. Reading about the lives of these workers who died more than two thousand years ago inspired me to write a story set in ancient Egypt.

GLOSSARY

akhet
The ancient Egyptians divided the year into three seasons. Akhet was the first season of the year when the Nile flooded.

amulet
Good luck charms worn by ancient Egyptians to protect them against disease and evil. Amulets were also wrapped inside a mummy's bandages to give good luck to the dead person as they travelled through the underworld.

cubit
The cubit was the main measurement of distance in ancient Egypt. It was the average length of a man's arm from his elbow to the tips of his fingers, 52.5 cm.

deben
A unit of weight somewhere between 90 and 100 grams.

Horus eye

Horus was the hawk-god of ancient Egypt.
Horus lost an eye in a battle, but the goddess
Hathor restored it. His eye became a symbol
of healing and is used in many paintings
and sculptures.

lapis lazuli

A dark blue semi-precious stone which the
Egyptians considered to be more valuable
than any other stone because it was the
same colour as the heavens.

palm-width

The average width of the palm of an Egyptian
man's hand, 7.5 cm.

papyrus

A plant with tall, triangular shaped stems that
grows in marshy ground. Ancient Egyptians
made a kind of paper from the dried stems of
this plant.

peret
The season of spring.

sarcophagus
A large stone container, usually rectangular, made to house a coffin.

senet
A board game played by ancient Egyptians. It involved two players each with seven pieces and was played on a rectangular board divided into thirty squares. Archaeologists have found many senet boards in tombs, but haven't been able to work out what the rules of the game were.

stele (plural stelae)
A slab of stone or wood with an inscription or painting on it used in funerals. The stele had prayers to the gods on them, often mentioning all the offerings and worship that the dead person had given to the gods when he or she was alive.

underworld, afterlife

The ancient Egyptians believed that the earth
was a flat disc. Beneath the earth was the
underworld, a dangerous place. After they
died Egyptians believed they had to first pass
through the underworld before they could live
forever in the afterlife.

vizier

A very important person. He was the pharaoh's
chief minister. He made sure that Egypt was run
exactly the way the pharaoh wanted it.

Return to Ancient Egypt for more exciting
adventures as Ramose continues his quest to be
restored to his rightful place – heir to the throne
of Egypt.

The Third Book in the Ramose Series

RAMOSE: STING OF THE SCORPION

The Fourth Book in the Ramose Series

RAMOSE: THE WRATH OF RA

The Second Book in the Ramose Series

RAMOSE AND THE TOMB ROBBERS

Everyone thinks Ramose is dead and buried, but he is alive and trying to stay that way. He must expose those who tried to murder him and regain his position as Pharaoh's rightful heir.

But Ramose has been kidnapped by tomb robbers – who will force him to lead them to the hidden treasures of the royal tombs. He will be killed as soon as he is of no use. He'll need more than the luck of the gods to get out of this one.

About the Author

Carole Wilkinson is an award-winning writer of over thirty books and TV scripts. She is interested in the history of everything and finds the hardest thing about writing books is to stop doing the research. She collects teapots and lives in Melbourne, Australia, with her husband, daughter and a spotty dog called Mitzie.

For Maryann and Andrew

R HMOSE

INCE IN EXILE

CAROLE WILKINSON